FORGOTTEN ROMANCE

DIVORCED MEN'S CLUB
BOOK 6

SAXON JAMES

AUTHOR'S NOTE

Well, this is it!

The final book in my Divorced Men's Club series.

I'm blown away by the support you've shown for these guys. Beau and Payne were complete buttheads to write, but they were my first book that really proved I could turn the ideas in my head into a career.

I want to take this moment to thank you for supporting me and for loving the guys. This series has been so much fun and it's bittersweet to say goodbye to Kilborough and the DMC.

As Art would say: we end one thing so we can begin another.

I hope you're all excited for what might be next!

As with all of my books, Forgotten Romance has been through a rigorous editing process, but ninja typos are a thing! If you spot any, please don't use kindle's reporting feature as it can have author accounts flagged. If you're someone who likes to pass them on though, you're more than welcome to email: admin@saxonjamesauthor.com.

This will ensure none of those corrections are missed with file updates.

Thanks so much for reading!

PROLOGUE

Mack

When my husband, Davey, finally walks in our front door, it's close to 2:00 a.m. He tries to sneak, pushing the door closed carefully, before standing his suitcase next to it and toeing out of his shoes.

My chest hurts just watching him. Everything about him is so familiar, and I miss it. Every day. We met close to twenty years ago, on his visit home after graduating college, and I've been consumed by him ever since. I wish we could go back to that. To the days when things were fun and easy and I didn't have this bowling-ball-sized lump constantly sitting on my chest.

Davey turns and stumbles to a stop when he sees me. "Mack? Baby, I said don't wait up."

My face screws up against the need to cry through the anger burning me. "Why are you so late?"

"Flight was delayed." His voice sounds wrecked. He's definitely tired, but so am I. So tired. Not because it's late, but because I'm married to a man who's never home, who looks after his family by working himself into the ground, and who leaves me to explain to our kids where Daddy is.

I miss him so much it hurts.

But I'm *tired*.

"Well, it had to be something, right?" I ask, not trying to mask the hurt.

Davey rubs his temples, and I recognize the way his shoulders go stiff. "Mack … I can't do this right now."

"Do what? I'm not doing anything."

He drops down onto the couch across from me, and I can't hold in the thoughts I've sat with for the last six hours.

"Just saying that it's becoming more and more common for you to get stuck at work these days. Or to miss your flight. Or to have to duck into the office or to take a call." My throat is getting thick. "Or maybe it's not work keeping you away at all."

He sighs, looking at his hands and not me. "Please don't do this again."

"Well, there has to be some reason why you don't want to be home with us."

"Are you fucking kidding?" he snaps, like I knew he would. I know my husband so well by now that pushing his buttons is easy, and usually I do it to get the amazing makeup sex that comes with it, but I don't think that's what it is this time.

This time, I don't even know what I want.

"I always want to be home with you," Davey says. "It *kills* me to leave you and the kids, but it's my *job*. Why don't you get that?"

"Because you could have any job. And you choose the one that means you're gone half of the time. You dump everything on me, pack your bag, and go, then expect me to be okay with that. It might have worked when it was just us, but the kids don't understand. Having to do everything myself is too much."

"You know how much I love what I do. You know how hard I've worked for this."

"Yeah, well, I didn't realize you love it more than you love us."

I know I've gone too far the second the words are out of my mouth.

Am I being an asshole? Yes.

Is it long past needing to be said? Also yes.

"That's not fair."

"Not *fair*? What's not fair is only having a husband half of the time. The kids only having Daddy when Daddy wants to be around."

"Mack …"

"We don't even have sex anymore. Do you know it's been six months? Six whole fucking months, from the man who couldn't keep his hands off me when we met."

"Is that what this is about? You want to have sex more?"

My nostrils flare because he doesn't get it. I married Davey because he made me feel like I was his entire world, but little by little, that world was taken away from me and given to his work. I want to have a husband who loves me. Who's so excited to get home to see me that he'd never miss his flight. Never want to be away a week at a time in the first place. Why can't he be as obsessed with me as I am with him?

I swallow roughly, dreading asking my next question. I've

thrown it at him in fits of rage before, but this might be the only time I've meant it. "Is there someone else?"

"Someone else? Come on, Mack."

"That wasn't a no."

"Because why the hell would you ask that in the first place? I love you. I love our kids. I'm sitting here being told I'm a shitty dad and husband, and now you're asking if I'm cheating on you?" He presses his fingers into his eye sockets. "I … Every time. Every time I get home lately. Every, single, damn time. I can't keep doing this. I'm exhausted."

"Try being a single parent."

He jolts like I've hit him. "Ouch."

I blink, spilling tears onto my cheeks. "I'm sorry. It's … I can't … I need my husband."

"You have me."

"No, I don't. You think it hurts you to leave? Every time you walk out the door, it's like my heart's being ripped out. You say you love me, but I haven't felt it in a really long time. And I'm so damn sick of staying awake all night, not knowing where you are and who you're with and if this will be the time you come home and say you've had enough of me."

"But you're saying you've had enough of *me*?"

My knees are bouncing up and down, because am I? I don't know. I don't have a solution. I'm scared and confused. I'm sick of feeling sick.

"All I know is that I can't keep going like this."

"You know I've tried to find something else, but nothing has been a good fit."

Maybe he did, maybe he didn't. The last year has been a blur. "It's too much."

"What are you saying?"

"Maybe … If you can't give up work … maybe you need

to give up us." My heart strangles at the words, but maybe this is what he needs. Maybe this will be the wake-up call for Davey to realize what matters most in life. He's amazing at what he does, he earns bucketloads of money, but we don't need all that. We just need him home again.

"What are you saying?"

"We both can't do this anymore, so …"

"Are you … are you saying you want a divorce?"

A *divorce*? Holy fuck, that sounds final. But if I'm going to push him back to us, I need to follow through. A divorce sounds exactly like the kind of world-ending finality he needs to take a step back and look at what he's doing to us. "I … I think so."

Davey breaks down into tears, and I'm not far behind him. I love him so fucking much, want to spend my whole fucking life with him, and if he feels anything even close to what I do, he'll make the right choice.

He'll choose us.

I give him all the time he needs for how serious this is to sink in.

Davey stands from the couch and pulls me up and into his arms. He holds me tight, crushes me to him, and we cry together for so long I almost forget what I'm crying about. Almost.

And when he pulls back, I wait for him to tell me he'll fix it. He'll sort something out with his job. He'll be here for us.

But when he opens his mouth, those aren't the words that come.

"If that's what you want, then okay. I'll look into how we do it in the morning."

A rush echoes in my ears, and I realize it's the sound of my life completely falling apart.

1

Davey

Two Years Later

My gut is tied in knots as I take a car from the airport to home, still reeling that I have an entire twelve weeks ahead with my family.

The last time this happened was … never. For the last eight years, I've been working my ass off for Dayton PR with two straight weeks in the office, followed by two weeks working from home, and now … the promotion to marketing director has never felt so good. Negotiating leave for Christmas and extended remote work for the holiday period was hard-won, but goddamn it, I was determined.

My head swims at the freedom these next three months

will bring. Home with my kids and my husband—*ex*-husband. I shake my head, hoping the reminder will sink in this time. The divorce was amicable, it was what Mack needed, but everything has been so complicated since.

I should have at least moved out of the family home, but with Van and Kiera still so young and me home only half of the month, it didn't make sense to get my own place where my time with them would be even more limited.

So I'd stayed.

Moved as far as the spare room, and every time I'm home, I develop the deepest kind of insomnia, thinking about Mack, asleep in our bed on the other side of the wall.

I swallow roughly, gripping the bag at my feet tighter. It's filled to the bursting with Christmas gifts, even though I know Mack more than has it covered, but every day I've been gone this last month, I've been thinking about them.

My son, my daughter, my *ex*-husband. Those three will always be the world to me, no matter how legally separated we are. No matter how much Mack might think I put my work first. Everything I do, it's always for them.

The car pulls up out the front of our home, and the warmth I get every time I'm here never fails to catch me off guard. Deep peace settles into my bones, and I get to live with that feeling for three whole fucking months. Nothing to take me away. Nothing to split my attention.

My grin spreads across my face as I jump out and meet the driver at the trunk, where he's already pulling my suitcase out.

"Thanks so much."

He flicks me a wave, jumps back in the car, and takes off.

I turn back to the house and catch two little faces popping up in the window curiously. Their eyes land on me, and Kiera's whole face lights up.

"Daddy!" I'm not sure if I can actually hear her over the breeze or if her voice is embedded in my brain, but the second her lips form the word, Van's little face lights up too, and they both disappear.

I jog for the front door and reach it just as Kiera throws it open and jumps into my arms. Van clings to my leg, and I scoop him up too, taking a minute to squeeze the ever-loving shit out of them. Van wriggles in my grip, stuttering out a barely formed sentence that I have no hope of understanding.

I raise my eyebrows at Kiera. "What did he say?"

"He wants to show you his trucks."

Well, thank goodness for that. I thought he'd said something about fucks.

"Davey?"

I set the kids down, using the moment to steady myself before glancing up at Mack. My smile isn't anywhere near as insane as it was for the kids, but it's there anyway. How this man can make me both so happy and so fucking sad at the same time, I'll never know. "Don't tell me you've forgotten what I look like already."

He rolls his eyes and meets me in the hall, where he hauls me into a hug. "We didn't think you'd be home until next week."

My hands find the place on his lower back where they fit so well. "I know." Him being happy to see me has me feeling smug. "I wanted to surprise you."

"We're surprised." He steps back suddenly, breaking the amazing contact between us, and that's the last chance I'll get to hold him again until I leave.

Van tugs at my arm. "Fuck. Fuck."

"Well, that's new," I say to Mack.

He looks bewildered. "It's truck. I swear."

"Big fuck. *Biiig* fuck. See. See."

"Go let him show you," Mack says. "I'll take your stuff up to …" He clears his throat, and I know he'd been about to say *our room*. "I'll take it up."

"Thanks."

I follow Van into the living area, where toys are spilled all across the rug. The mostly empty bowls from their dinner are sitting on the coffee table, where they've clearly just finished eating, and it's a way too obvious reminder of them going on with their lives without me.

It's hard to be grateful for three months when Mack gets to have this always.

I wonder if he knows how lucky he is?

Van and I zoom cars around on the floor while Kiera grabs one of her schoolbooks to show me all the art she's working on. I missed her first day of kindergarten, which killed me, but thankfully, kids are kids, and that's not something she probably even thinks about.

A bowl of stir-fry is set down beside me, and my stomach immediately growls.

"Figured you'd be hungry after that flight," Mack says. "I know how much you hate airplane food."

"It's the worst," I moan, snatching up the bowl. Fuck, I love Mack's cooking. It's nothing fancy or special, but it tastes like home. "Damn, this is so good."

Mack's cheeks take on that pinkness that I love as he rubs a hand over his lips, trying not to smile. "It's noodles and sauce from the packet. All I did was cook the meat and throw it all together."

"No one knows how to throw prepackaged ingredients together like you do—" I cut off before I can call him baby.

I'd thought that it would get easier. That after the divorce papers were official, it would sink in that he's not mine anymore, and I'd find it easier to move on. I even made a dating profile and everything.

The problem is, he's still my best friend. It's always awkward when I first get home and right before I leave again, like my presence disrupts the dust of our relationship and the reasons for our fights. But once the awkwardness fades, it goes back to how it's always been between us. Easy. Light. He's my favorite person.

It's why I keep ignoring that voice telling me I need to make other arrangements.

"So …" He sits on the arm of the couch, crossing his arms and his legs at the ankle. "You're home early. What does that mean for Christmas? Will you be here?"

Given that every year, I only get two weeks off, I'm not surprised that he's asking. It does hurt that he thinks potentially missing Christmas with my family—especially when the kids are at such a fun age—is something I'd do.

"You have to be," Kiera cuts in. "How will Santa know where to leave your presents if you're not at home?"

I poke her belly. "I'll be here. I wouldn't want Santa forgetting about me, after all."

"You will?" The hope in Mack's eyes gets me right in the chest, and I know he's trying to calculate. It's the start of November; if I'm here for two weeks, gone for two weeks, then back home for two, that would mean that I'd be gone over the holidays. We have a lot to talk about.

"Yeah," I croak. "I got some extended time at home."

"How long?"

"Twelve weeks. I've done a lot for the company, and it's about time they gave me something back."

"Twelve … weeks?" Mack doesn't look as thrilled as I'd been hoping for. "Huh. Okay."

"Is that a problem?"

"*No*. No problem. It's just …"

"The longest time we've spent together since before we got married?"

His clear blue eyes meet mine, all wide and unguarded. "Exactly."

"I won't get in your way, don't worry. But I'll be here to take some of the stress off your shoulders for a bit."

He bites at this thumbnail. "And at the end of the twelve weeks, you'll go again?"

"Well, yeah. That's my job."

His lips turn down.

"Hey, I thought this would be a good thing."

"Yeah, I know," he mutters. "That's the problem."

My good mood crashes. "You don't want me here?"

He opens his mouth but snaps it shut again. "It's fine. We'll be fine."

"Fine?"

"And this is a picture I did of a reindeer!" Kiera shrieks, holding up a scribbled body that almost looks like it could be some kind of animal.

"Wow," I say as Mack disappears into the kitchen. "How did you get so talented?"

"Lots and lots of practice."

I hand over the little car I'm playing with and kiss her on the hair. "Play with Van for a minute?"

She drops down onto the carpet, and I go through to where Mack is gripping the edge of the sink.

"Tell me what's wrong."

"I don't wanna …"

"Mack, come on."

He shakes his head. "You'll feel bad."

"Yeah, well, thinking my hu—*you* don't want me around is sort of already doing that." I watch as he takes a deep breath and lets it out before turning to me.

"They're always so upset when you leave. And that's after only a few weeks. What will months be like?"

Well, way to make the guilt hit hard.

"What are you saying? Do you want me to leave?"

He looks horrified. "Of course not."

"Then move out, or … is it going to be too hard for you?"

"No, I don't want you to go."

"Then what is it?"

He gives me those big, sweet puppy dog eyes that never fail to melt me. "I don't want you to *go*."

And there it is. The one and only problem between us that ended up being too big to fix.

"Yeah," I say, rubbing my knuckles over a knot in the wooden kitchen cabinet. "Some days, neither do I." He lights up, and I hurry to continue. "But I have to. You know that."

"Right."

We linger in a prolonged silence.

"It's bedtime," he finally says. "You want to do the story?"

2

Mack

Me:

SOS.

SOS. SOS. SOS.

The second Davey is nestled upstairs with the kiddies, my official freak-out begins.

Three *months*? I get him home for three whole stinking months? Maybe if I can make the next three months the best they've ever been, if I'm sweet and romantic and look after him, if I remind him how things always were together, this will be my chance. A life that good is too hard to walk away from twice. Right?

The group chat has not reacted to my distress signal, which is, quite frankly, rude and insulting.

I skip the fun of keeping them in suspense because I'm

bursting with energy and a plan, and I need to get it all out. Now. Immediately.

My phone lights up with a call from Art. He's one of my closest friends and was happily playing the field before Joey made him fall head over tit.

"Hello?"

"What's the emergency?"

I grin. "I'm going to win my husband back."

There's complete silence, and I check the call is still connected. Then, Art says one word.

"No."

I halt, head in the freezer, as I look to see if we have the ingredients for the casserole Davey likes. "No *what*?"

"You will not be doing that."

A little of my excitement dims. "Why not?"

"Because," Art says patiently. "It goes completely against our current plan, which is to get you dating again. What happened to Luke?"

I think of the guy I went out with once and who's texted me a few times. Our one and only date ended up with me in the hospital from anaphylaxis. "We, uh, haven't caught up again. No good time. I'm very busy."

"Mack, it's me. Cut the shit."

"Fine. I don't want to go out with him."

"Okay, then. We'll find someone else. Plenty of fish in the sea and all that. Maybe you can take a leaf out of Griff's book —got any best friends I can push you together with?"

"Yes. Davey."

His sigh is less patient than his words. "You're divorced. For a good reason."

"But what if—"

"No."

"But—"

"Mack. No. We've been over this." He groans. "Look, I'm only going to say this once because I will support whatever you choose to do, but you know that if you go through with this plan, you're going to get hurt. Davey is going to leave again. I love the guy, I loved you two for each other, but I'm friends with him too, and I know a workaholic when I see one. He loves his job. You made him choose once, and he did. You won't survive coming second again."

I swallow around the lump building in my throat. "I know. But I have to try."

"Okay. I tried. I said my piece. If that's your choice, what do you need me to do?"

"Really?" The fact he switched sides like that so quickly makes me think this could actually work. "You'll help?"

"Of course. Nothing shady, but I'm a good sounding board, and I'm romantic as fuck. Ask Joey."

There's a murmured voice in the background.

"Ah, actually, don't ask Joey," Art says. "I'm your friend, and they basically call me Casanova—that should be evidence enough."

There's more I can't make out from Joey in the background before Art continues.

"Again, do *not* ask Joey. He's very busy with schoolwork and being locked in my sex dungeon."

"I miss sex."

Art chuckles. "I have tried many times to fix that for you, but my blow job offer is officially off the table. I happen to like my balls still attached to my body."

"That's fine. I don't know where your mouth has been anyway," I say absently as I hear Davey's footsteps on the stairs. "I've gotta go," I hiss into the phone.

"In that case, I will begin plotting the worst idea ever. Talk soon."

I hurry to hang up as Davey rounds the corner into the kitchen. It always throws me how perfectly he fits into the house and my life. He's never out of place, and the urge to walk over and wrap my arms around him, to back him laughingly into the wall as I try to steal all the kisses I can, is strong.

Instead, I shove my hands into my pockets.

"They asleep?"

"I didn't even get to finish the book." He walks over to the sink to wash his hands. "There was something sticky in Van's bed."

"Huh. I guess that's where the candy cane went."

"Candy cane?"

I wave the question off. "Want to watch a movie?"

Davey's face lights up, and it makes me smile back automatically. "Yeah, what were you thinking?"

"Anything that doesn't have kids' characters in it works for me."

"I might just duck out and check on my—"

"Your LEGO?" I grin. "It's fine. It's always fine. The kids aren't allowed out there without you, and I give it a dust every Sunday night."

"You've been looking after it?"

"With how long it took you to build that spaceship and all the cursing and late nights, of course. I can't go through that again."

Davey laughs and grabs two cans of Coke out of the fridge.

He follows me through to the living room, where we both scoop up handfuls of little cars to toss inside the bucket I keep them in. Then we flop down on the couch, side by side, and it's exactly the same as it ever was.

"You work tomorrow?" he asks as I flip through the options, looking for something interesting.

"Yep. I'll drop the kids at school and then go in."

"I can do it if you like? Just get yourself ready."

That will make things easier. "Sweet, thanks." I debate over asking about his work, but how can I not? It's the most important part of his life … for now. Even if I want to kill it with fire. "How's the promotion going?"

"Eh, you don't want to hear about that."

"Of course I do. It makes you happy." And I'll stop talking there because perfect husband Mack doesn't do bitterness. Only support and all things positive. Davey's number one fan.

"It's sort of strange to have a team reporting to me."

"Really? But haven't you done a lot of that anyway?"

"Yes and no. Before, I was part of the team. Part of coming up with the ideas and things … now, people bring the promotion packages to me to go over."

Dammit, it sounds exactly like the type of thing Davey would love. This is going to be harder than I thought. Doesn't matter. I just have to try even harder.

"Sounds stressful to me."

"Well, yeah." He turns his head to give me a soft smile, and this close, his dark freckles are more prominent in the glow of the TV. I've kissed those freckles too many times to count, and I dream about doing it again. "We're very different people."

"Not that different." The response is immediate and doesn't make sense, considering we always used to joke about being each other's missing piece. Davey loves traveling, he's organized, sensible, calms down with LEGO, and loves a good challenge. I love nothing more than settling at home, either reading or playing video games, and being goofy with my friends and family.

I don't want serious. I don't want a jet-setting life.

I want the kids and Davey and my job at the library. That's it.

"Oh yeah?" he asks, turning to prop his elbow on the back of the couch. "What's the same about us?"

"We, uh … like stir-fry."

Davey's eyes twinkle. "What else? Not food related."

My heartbeat quickens at being the sole focus of his attention. How many other men have sat across from him like this over the last two years and got to witness being in the best place on earth?

Still, it's a sad couple of minutes when the only other things I can think of are the kids and sex.

Stir-fry, our kids, and sex.

The three things we have in common, and they're shaky at best. We have to love our kids, and food and sex aren't exactly strong building blocks of a relationship. Maybe our problem was never his work at all. Maybe it's that we're too different.

I'm scrambling to come up with goddamn anything, and that teasing light is fading from Davey's face.

Am I an idiot? Just an idealistic moron thinking I can single-handedly fix this all because we have more time together?

The problem is that I can't *not* believe that because if I do, it means admitting this thing between us is over. It can't be. I refuse to let us grow apart until we don't even have this anymore.

Davey's the only man for me, and I really hope he'll remember I'm the only man for him.

I just have to *make* him remember.

Three months, and I'll shower him with all the love in the world. Starting tomorrow, there's no more ex-husbands, only us. If I want to hug him, I will. If I want to do something nice for him, I will. Davey is going to be smothered in affection unless he tells me to stop because this divorce was never supposed to happen. He was supposed to fight for me.

So now, I'm going to do what I should have done back then. Even if I fail.

"We're both stubborn mules," I finally say. Whether it's his LEGO or my games or the way we're raising the kids. Everything down to the divorce I want to forget about.

Neither of us wants to lose.

If I can get him fighting for us too, nothing will stop us.

3

Davey

I'M AWAKE BEFORE THE REST OF THE HOUSE, THANKS TO THE last two weeks of getting up early to get in to the office. It's a weird feeling, lying in bed when my natural instinct is to jump up, make a big pot of coffee, and start making my way through my full inbox. I'm so used to every free moment being spent on the move, brain occupied with problem-solving and new ideas.

Being still, not having to fill every minute with work that feels like it's never finished … I never learned how to do that.

My memories stray back to waking up next to Mack and his mouth breathing. He runs naturally cold, so without a doubt, every night, he'd steal the blankets, and by morning, he'd be wrapped in an impenetrable cocoon, and I'd be plastered up against him, trying to steal some of his warmth.

My hands run over the bedding, still lying neat and straight over the top of me, hating how unnatural it looks. I kick the blankets off and slide my feet into my waiting slippers before heading downstairs to turn the heat on. It's cold enough this year that we could be heading for a white Christmas. We haven't had one since before Van was born, and there's nothing more magical to me than looking outside on Christmas Eve and seeing the snow fall.

It's about the only time of year I can stand the stuff.

I get myself a coffee but make a conscious effort to leave my phone behind as I walk into the back room off the kitchen. We enclosed it when we first bought the house so we could make use of it in winter too. It has a clear view out to the woods behind the house, and to the left, I can make out one side of Kil Pen sitting high on the mountain.

I try to imagine this being my life. Waking early, drinking coffee in the quiet, no job to get to … Taking Mack and the kids out of that picture, it seems … boring. Fuck.

I bury one hand in my curls and sip my drink. This is the problem. I know that giving up my job and being here permanently would go a long way toward fixing things between us, but how do I do that when I know that it will make me miserable? At some point, I'd end up resenting him. I never, ever want that for us.

The thing is, I truly believe that to be in a strong relationship, you need to have strength in who you are outside of it. If you're not your own person, with your own goals and life, what the hell can you offer your partner?

Do I wish I could travel less? Of course. But I've worked so damn hard for my career that I can't throw it all away. Especially because we *need* the money I'm bringing in, and with how the economy is going down the shitter, I'm always terrified of the world Van and Kiera are inheriting. If I can build a sizable nest egg for them, it's a sacrifice I have to make.

Even if my whole life's trajectory outside of work makes me miserable as fuck.

I sigh and down my coffee, then head into the kitchen to get Kiera's school lunch ready. I pull out clothes for her and Van, and then, on a whim, I grab Mack's favorite work shirt and the pants that make his butt look edible and throw them in the dryer to warm up before he puts them on.

The shower comes on upstairs, letting me know he's up too, and I smile a little over him expecting to come down and scramble around getting everything ready when I'm all over it. I might only be here half of the time, but when I'm here, I make sure to pull my weight.

I grab the clothes from the dryer and sneak upstairs into the room we used to share, ignoring the pang it sets off behind my sternum. Then, I fold his warm clothes and set them at the foot of his bed before sneaking out again.

It's only a few minutes later that what can only be an elephant stampede thunders down the stairs. The TV comes on, and then Mack appears, hair wet, eyes reddened, probably from having as crappy of a sleep as I had.

His face lights up with a smile when he spots me, and then he surprises the hell out of me by setting his hand on my waist to get around me to the coffeepot. "Warm clothes and fresh coffee?" He moans sinfully. "Morning in heaven."

Then my heart goddamn stops when he wraps an arm around me and presses his lips to my temple. Mack moves on like it's nothing out of the ordinary, and maybe two years ago, it wasn't, but that … it's been so long since I've had casual affection from him that I'm momentarily stunned.

"Sleep well?" I ask, stumbling over my question.

"Like a baby."

"Huh." I glance at his bloodshot eyes and away again. It's not my place to ask. "Busy day at work?"

Mack lights up like he always does, and I wonder if that's what I look like when I talk about work. "We've got the mini lit program on this morning, and this afternoon, Wheedling and Needling had a room booked. I swear their knitting club is more for gossip than anything else. They could give Art a run for his money."

"I'm surprised he's not part of that club." I chuckle, thinking of Art de Almeida getting wrapped up in yarn as the old ladies fuss over him.

"What are you going to do today?" Mack asks.

He doesn't normally ask, so I hesitate before answering. I'll probably check in on work, even though I don't have to, but the last thing I want to do is ruin a good morning talking about something he hates. "I'll go for a walk until my balls feel like they're freezing off and then visit some people. Mind if I drop you at work and take the car?"

"Fine by me."

We have breakfast together and get the kids dressed, and as Mack darts upstairs to finish getting ready, there's a knock at the door.

I open it to find a cute redheaded guy huddled into the scarf around his neck.

"Davey, right?" he asks, smiling at me.

"Ah, right …" I look him over, getting a bad feeling about this. "Sorry, I don't think I know you."

"Oh, Luke." He holds out his gloved hand, and I can't do anything but shake it.

"Hey …"

He doesn't look anywhere near as awkward as I feel as he

scuffs his sneaker on our front step and glances into the house. "Is, uh, Mack home?"

And there it is. The source of my intense discomfort. "He is."

Luke waits me out a moment. "Can I see him?"

Fuck. This is like an awkward boyfriend meeting the parents, only worse because I used to fuck the guy he's waiting to see. "I … guess …"

"Luke?" Mack asks.

I turn around to find him looking like a fucking snack. He's done his hair, he smells incredible, and those pants are fitting in all the delicious ways I remember. I consider for one wild moment jumping in front of him with a blanket to shield him from view but decide against it. Might look a bit desperate.

"Hey, Mack." Luke looks over-fucking-joyed. "I was around this morning, and I thought … if you're free … maybe we could grab some breakfast?"

Mack's face falls, and he looks genuinely disappointed. "I can't today. I have to work."

"Ah, damn."

I clear my throat. "Speaking of work, we should get going." I spare Luke the most painful smile I can imagine. "We have to drop the kids off first, and we're cutting it tight for time."

"Well, why don't I give Mack a lift?"

Now who's looking fucking desperate? My teeth clack as I try to remember my patience and let him down easy. But Mack gets in there first.

"Could you? That would actually be a huge help." He lowers his voice slightly. "The kids' school is on the opposite side of town to the library."

"Yeah, it's no problem at all. I don't start work until noon, so I have time to kill. Hey—maybe I could duck out and grab breakfast and bring it to you."

"We've already had breakfast," I point out.

"Second breakfast, then. Or elevensies." Luke laughs, and Mack's eyes widen.

"Tell me you're referencing *The Hobbit*."

"Of course."

"I love that book."

"I know. You mentioned it on our date, like, twenty times." Luke leans over toward me like he's letting me in on a secret. "I've only seen the movie."

Mack shakes his head in horror. "We're going to have to fix that."

I'm sorry—*we*?

My heart beats louder as I glance between the two of them.

Luke's here. At our house. They've been on a date. He knows *The Hobbit*, which I fell asleep through all three times Mack tried to watch it with me. The panic bubbling in my gut is chasing away the chill from outside, and all I can do is watch as Mack grabs his bag, ducks inside to squeeze Van and Kiera goodbye, and then disappears out the door with Luke.

No casual hug. No kiss on the temple.

Only a fast smile and the back of his head as he walks away and climbs into Luke's car.

"Who's that, Daddy?" Kiera asks, waving as Mack leaves.

"A … friend. Of Dad's." I pause, knowing I shouldn't ask but doing it anyway. "Have you met that friend before?"

"No. Why does his hair look like fire?"

A tiny bit of the knot growing in my gut loosens. "It's the color. Go brush your teeth."

Kiera runs off, and I slump against the doorframe. I'm not sure why Mack dating catches me so completely off guard, considering we've been separated for two years now, but I feel like I've been winded. I might need to talk to him about random men showing up at the door when I'm home, because fuck. I'd never do that to him. Throw someone new in his face.

I guess with the kids and us still living together, I'd always taken for granted that things wouldn't change. We're not together, but … we are. In a way.

Luke ruins everything.

He's the glass shattering on my comfortable life, and it feels like I've swallowed gravel as I get Van and Kiera to the car and strap them in. Is this what the next twelve weeks will be like? Having to watch my husband go out with other men?

Maybe … maybe it's time. It doesn't make financial sense to get my own place here, but what the fuck am I supposed to do? Lie in my bed, listening to Mack next door with someone else?

Or worse—him not coming home at all.

I scrub at my eyes before turning the car on.

None of this is Mack's fault.

None is mine either.

We both just wanted different things.

But why the hell does one of those things have to be *Luke*?

4

Mack

"I take three days off and have to be told by *Rhonda* about you being dropped off by a man folk on Monday." Tonya fans herself. "Apparently, he was quite the catch. A regular Mr. Darcy."

I laugh at her dramatics and continue rehoming the cart of books beside me. You'd think with being almost twenty years older than us and the manager here that Rhonda would have more important things to be doing than gossiping. Apparently not. "Just a …" I pause, because *friend* doesn't sound right. Other than our date, a few texts, and the other morning, we haven't had much to do with each other. I declined breakfast with the excuse I needed to work, but if I'm honest, it felt too weird.

Luke is great, but I don't want to lead the poor guy on.

"Uh-*huh*." Tonya gets a coy smile. "A … lover? Hottie? Boyyyfriend?"

"None of those." I frown. "I was going to say friend, but can he be called that when I barely even know the guy?"

"Know as in know or know as in *knooow*?"

"Please stop."

She sobers up. "What's wrong? You know I'm only teasing."

"I know, but Luke isn't like that. Also …" I play with the corner of the book I've just picked up. "Davey's home."

She snorts. "Goodie."

"For three months."

Her long exhale breezes through the quiet air around us. "Well. That's different."

"It's been so nice having him home and knowing he doesn't have to leave again in a few days."

"But … he will leave. Right?"

It's the undeniable truth that I don't want to face. I'm happy living in my own bubble of la-la land and would really like it if people could stop throwing reality at me. Reality sucks. Zero rating out of ten. Where are the mystical unicorns of possibility? Oh, that's right, they *died*.

Just straight up smother me in delulu, thank you.

"Not for a while," I say. "It'll be good for the kids."

"And what about you?"

"It will be good for me too." Having Davey home is always a godsend, and not only because I like looking at his butt.

"It's not healthy that you guys still live together."

"It makes the most sense."

"So you say." Tonya lightly grabs my arm. "We love you, Mack. We're like a family here, and I know you miss Davey, but Rhonda said this guy was all goo-goo eyes for you, and you deserve to have someone look at you like that."

"Davey used to look at me like that."

"But he doesn't anymore."

I gently shake her off. "Goo-goo eyes are all good in the beginning, but even if I did date Luke, he wouldn't look at me like that forever. Am I supposed to give up on my marriage because we're not silly idiots over each other anymore?"

She raises her eyebrows and looks at me in concern. "No … you're supposed to give up on your marriage when you're not *actually* married." She lifts her hands like she's surrendering. "I get it. Butt out."

"Thank you." It occurs to me she's not the only one lately who's given up on trying to warn me away from Davey. It'd be nice if I could find someone who was one hundred percent on my side. Art is supportive, but it's against his better judgment, so I don't feel completely okay confiding in him.

I think of some of my other friends in the divorced men's group that Art and Barney started. They're all awesome, but Davey is friends with most of them as well, so it's a delicate topic. Payne is anti-marriage after his first one went to hell. Griff would rather talk about sex than romance, and Keller is way too logical. His advice would be to flat out *ask* Davey if there's any chance there, but that would never work. I need to be sneakier than that. Cleverer. Davey needs to come to the realization that he needs us himself.

Orson could potentially be team Mack, but I don't think he'd want to go behind Davey's back with it.

What's the world coming to that a guy can't even get his friends on board with a little parent trap romancing? If only Van and Kiera were older. They'd be all too eager to lock us away for a romantic dinner together.

Probably.

The people I work with have heard too much about my heartbreak after the divorce to be Team Davey either. I'd started work here not long after the ink dried on those contracts, needing something to distract me from the shithole my life had fallen into. I knew I should have bottled all those feelings up instead. Damn those healthy emotional habits.

So now I have no one to talk to, when all I need is just one person in my corner, cheering me on, telling me I can do it, and talking me through the noise when I start getting doubty.

I'm sure Davey is my person, so why is it so fucking hard to find one other person who thinks so as well?

I finish sorting the books, then help set up for the princess tea party we're having this morning. Seeing all the little kids come in with their princess dresses and tiaras makes me miss when Kiera would come to these every week with me. A lot of the themed ideas we have were started because I'd been looking for things for her to do, and our library memberships have been at a record high since.

Books are a big part of my life, but bringing the community together is why I'm here. The tea party takes up most of my morning, then Trent Briller comes in just before lunchtime, wanting to talk history as he loads up on World War Two books, and after he's done, Rhonda needs my help to hold a ladder while she climbs up and dusts off the top of the shelves.

No matter how many times I try to remind her she's fifty-nine, she steadfastly refuses to let me do it, so I end up hovering awkwardly under her, ready to play catch the granny.

I'm not confident in my chances of stopping us both from crashing to the floor though. By the time she climbs down again and pats me on the shoulder in thanks, there's stale sweat at my hairline and prickling my back.

Apparently, people gambling with death stresses me out, who knew?

I stop by the front desk to grab my coat and head out for lunch when I pause at the book resting innocently on the table. It's a shiny new copy of *The Hobbit*, and there's a piece of paper sticking out of the top of it.

I tug the paper out and read the handwritten note.

MACK,

What's a hobbit's favorite outing?
Going to the Frodeo!

A SMILE SPRINGS TO MY FACE.

YOU'RE WORTH MORE THAN WHAT A HOBBIT SPENDS ON FOOD each week.

From, your secret admirer.

MY SECRET ADMIRER? IS THIS A JOKE? GIVEN THE BOOK AND the note, I'd say it's not so secret. Still, even if I'm not interested in Luke like that … happy vibes come alive in my gut. It's nice. The attention and knowing that someone thinks that highly of me.

I'm walking a little taller as I head down the street in search of food.

It's too bad I'm so madly in love with Davey because Luke has a good heart. I'll have to let him know that when I make it clear I'm not interested because he'll make someone very happy one day, and I don't want him to think my lack of interest is anything he's done.

In fact, if it wasn't for Davey, that little note would have me messaging him right now to meet up.

It was cute. Very cute.

I can't remember the last time a man showed interest in me; I forget how it's all even supposed to work.

Instead of messaging Luke though, I pull out my phone and message Davey instead.

I'M HEADING FOR LUNCH. WHAT ARE YOU DOING?

HE TEXTS BACK ALMOST INSTANTLY.

AT KILLER BREW CATCHING UP WITH ART. COME JOIN US?

HMM … LUNCH WITH COMPANY SOUNDS GOOD. LUNCH WITH my ex-husband who I'm trying to win back and the friend who knows all about my plan? Risky. What if Art lets something slip? Or if Joey shows up and gets in one of his teasing moods?

I shouldn't risk it, but on the other hand, I get to see Davey. Four hours has been four too many.

On my way.

I cut through the next street to the boardwalk and follow it from the quiet backstreets where the library is to the busier area in the middle of town where Killer Brew stands over-looking the water. It's an impressive building, made even more impressive with Kilborough Penitentiary looming over it in the background.

My nose is frozen by the time I step inside, and I'm so cold I almost forget to be nervous. Almost. Because the second my gaze drops to where Davey is sitting opposite Art in a booth, it hits me right on cue.

I just love him so much.

If my plan doesn't work, I'll kick myself for the rest of eternity for ever testing him with my stupid divorce suggestion. If I'd never brought it up, we'd still be together. Miserable, but together. After all, misery loves company, so why the hell shouldn't I forcefully tie us together in an unholy abomination of marital unrest?

Davey slides over toward the wall as soon as he sees me and pats the space right next to him. I'd been going to sit next to Art so I didn't look so obvious about my need to be close to him, but this takes the decision out of my hands.

As soon as I sit down, I breathe in his familiar cologne.

"What are you two up to?" I ask.

Art answers immediately. "Planning world domination. We're trying to decide if we should put you down as a sex slave or the one who writes about our heroic quest for supremacy."

My wide eyes swing from him to Davey.

Davey shrugs. "If it helps, my vote was firmly for you being our scribe."

"Wait. You were *actually* talking about that?"

Art blinks at me. "Is there another position you'd like instead? Universal leader is taken, but there might be something on our council of fuckery."

"No, I meant were you really talking about the world domination thing?"

"People have to have goals, Mack."

I'm still not sure if Art is serious or not.

"Council of fuckery?" Davey asks. "Is that what we voted on?"

"I voted, you lost."

"How does that work if it's one on one?"

"Oh, because I have Joey. So all my votes count as two."

"Well, I have Mack. He's automatically on my side." Davey turns to me. "Aren't you?"

"Of course."

Art bows his head solemnly. "Only the romance can form a bond so deep your universal power doubles."

I narrow my eyes at him. "Does that mean basically all our friends are more powerful than us?"

"Hell no." Art looks at me like I'm not making sense. "That only works when you're the supreme ruler of the galaxy."

"I thought it was universal leader?"

Art looks to Davey for support. "I don't think he understands this game."

"I understand." And because I can't help myself, I turn to Davey too. "It means we have to get remarried, and because that's love times two, you'd outrank Art."

Davey smirks. "Sounds like you're onto something."

"Okay, game over," Art shouts, slapping his hands on the table. "Order your food and get out."

"I think he expected us to worship him," I stage-whisper at Davey.

"Definite inferiority complex."

Art rolls his eyes and leaves us at the table.

I turn so I'm facing Davey.

"Didn't want me for a sex slave?" I tease.

"Call me protective or some shit."

"Just saying, you remember all those things I can do with my tongue."

Davey's eyes lock onto mine. "And that's *exactly* why I said no."

My heartbeat kicks up a notch as we sit there, watching each other. "Didn't want anyone else to know that, huh?"

"I'm sure plenty of other men know by now, but I don't need to hear about it."

It's on the tip of my tongue to tell him that no other men know. There's been no one since him, and the few times I've come close to that happening, I couldn't bring myself to go through with it. But then his MyMatch profile pops into my head, and the words die. Admitting I've been pathetically pining over him while he's been out there hooking up would only make things awkward for us both.

"I know exactly what you mean," I agree.

DMC GROUP CHAT

Art: Now is your one and only chance to claim your positions under me as universal leader.

Payne: Anytime you say "under me" I will have questions.

Mack: I'm the scribe, apparently.

Art: I don't think that's what I voted for you as.

Payne: What did you vote for him as?

Orson: Do you really want the answer to that question?

Payne: Shit. I fucked up. Don't answer me.

Art: Do you want to tell them, Mack, or should I?

Mack: I already told them. Scribe. And nothing else.

Art: …

Art: …

Art: …

Art: Does pretending to type so the little dots come up increase suspense or what?

Keller: We're already bored.

Art: Sex slave. Mack is our sex slave.

Griff: Why don't I get to be the sex slave?

Keller: I seriously worry about you, dude.

Mack: Position is all yours.

Art: No it's not. I make the decisions. I'm the universal leader, dammit.

Orson: You sure? You kinda sound like a toddler right now.

Art: That's it. No positions. None of you will survive my takeover. You're all doomed.

Mack: Oh, thank god.

Art: I'm so unappreciated in my generation.

5

Davey

"Hey, baby," Mom says, pulling me into a hug when I step inside. Van and Kiera take off to find Pa while Mom and I head for the kitchen. Every day after school pickup, I stop in here to see them, and since retiring, Dad is the best source for town gossip. Between the golf club, his old construction friends, the fishing group, and the people he's known for years, he's always one of the first to know everything about anyone.

And today, I'd kind of like to know who the man is sniffing around my husband.

"Mack still at work?" Mom asks, filling a teapot.

"Yeah, I'll grab him at four."

"I tell you, the knitting girls love him. Now, I'm not old enough to be one of them yet"—I snicker, earning myself a whip from the dish towel—"but sometimes those ladies are on school pickup, and they're always gushing about my son-in-law. The mothers too. Do you know he runs kids days at the library? Princess picnics and robot building and …" She waves a hand. "Very clever, that man. All these women lamenting that he's gay."

Well, that's offensive. I don't point that out to her, though, because my parents weren't exactly thrilled with me over the divorce. Dad tried to be neutral, but Mom took Mack's side, begging me through tears to quit my job and stay home with my family.

It hurt almost as much as when Mack did it.

I doubt my choice enough without everyone else putting their opinions in. I hate leaving my family, I hate what I've done to us, I hate that I lost the greatest husband in existence. But it was clearly going to happen either way.

Mack loves his job at the library. Dad loved the building industry, and Mom loves teaching so much she still does it two days a week when she could have easily retired when Dad did.

But me? I think I'm broken. I could live without the travel, but I fucking *love* what I do. The pressure-cooker contracts. The brainstorming. The putting together a package and seeing it transformed into something real. And now, I get to run a whole fucking team. My work keeps me busy. It keeps me social. It keeps my mind alive, and giving that up wouldn't be good for me. At least with how we are now, Mack and I still get along. We're still close and care about each other.

If I quit and wound up waiting tables at Killer Brew, would I still be the same guy without the job satisfaction? The short answer is no. That right there would ruin us.

"I guess I did gay men everywhere a favor by divorcing him, then," I say, trying to keep the bitter tone out.

Mom presses her lips tight, and I know she wants to call me an idiot again, but ever since I reminded her that *I'm* the one she gave birth to, she's switched tactics. No more putting me down. A whole lot of talking Mack up.

"I'm just saying," she tsks. "He's a beautiful man. Bakes cookies with the kids every week before he comes to visit."

"I know." I might be gone a lot, but I'm still very present in their lives. "And I also know the cookies taste like pure sugar and you throw them out when he leaves."

"We would never waste them like that." She checks the tea and mutters, "Not while we have hungry chickens out back."

I watch while she pours out tea, debating whether I should even bother bringing up Luke. It's dangerous territory, and I'm risking being snapped by the towel again, but I haven't been able to stop thinking about the guy for the past few days.

He was friendly. Too friendly. I mean, what new guy doesn't at least throw the *tiniest* bit of shade at the ex?

I know there's no way I'll be able to leave here without mining for information on him, and I have to pick Mack up in half an hour.

"Do you know someone called Luke Dawson?"

She frowns as she thinks. "Dawson … Not Sharon's boy?"

I shake my head. "He's new in town."

"How old?"

"Ah …" I have no idea, but he didn't look that much younger than us. "Mid to late thirties, I'd guess."

Her gaze sharpens on me. "Did you meet him through this app of yours?"

Here we go again. When Mack and I first got divorced, I thought the fastest way to move on would be to start meeting with other people. There wasn't a single one of them who could measure up to him, and that idea died quickly.

Mom huffs. "You know I bite my tongue, but why would you look at dating someone else from town when you have

Mack, right here, who'd take you back the second you gave up work?"

Well, on top of Luke being a pain in my ass, that plain pisses me off. "You know, most parents are proud of their kids for building a successful career."

"I'm nearing the end of my life—"

"You're *seventy*. Stop with the guilt trip."

"I'm only saying, I know what's important and what isn't." She points toward the back door. "Those two out there are important."

"Plenty of people don't have kids and are happy."

"Of course they are. They don't have to have frustrating conversations with dumbass children."

I pin her with a look. "I think we can move on now."

"Fletcher?" Mom yells.

A couple of seconds later, Dad pops his head in the back door. "Yes, honey?"

"You're needed."

Dad kicks off his boots and walks inside, throwing his thick jacket down on the back of the couch. "We're shoveling pig shit. What is it?"

"You do know Kiera and Van have to get back in my car, right?"

Dad looks completely unbothered.

Mom sighs. "Davey is asking about a boy."

"He's not a *boy*."

"Luke … something."

"Dawson."

Dad tilts his head, thinking for a second. "New guy round here? Red hair?"

Trust Dad to know. "That's him."

"What about him?"

Mom answers before I can. "Davey's interested in him."

"Goddamnit, woman. Not me. Mack."

Silence falls between the three of us, and I think it's because I got snappy, but I'm wrong.

"Mack's *dating*?" Mom shrieks.

"No. Well, maybe. This Luke guy's interested."

The pang in my chest only has a second to make itself known before Mom groans loudly.

"It's over."

"Mary …"

"No. All this time, I've been hoping you'll grow up. Stop taking trips all over the country and work out how good you have it here. How *good* you are with Mack, and now he's … he's …"

"Why do you think he's interested?" Dad asks, talking over the top of Mom.

I want to tell Mom to shut it, but she isn't saying anything I'm not already beating myself up over. "He showed up the other morning and offered Mack a lift to work. I could tell. Luckily we've left early the last two days, so I haven't had to see him again, but I get the feeling it's only a matter of time."

"Then you need to move fast," Mom says. "You're home for three whole months. Win your husband back."

"I'm not going to try and manipulate him into being with me again. Especially when nothing's changed."

I can read every reply going on behind her eyes. *Then change it. Quit your job. Put your family first.* But my job *is* putting my family first. Our mortgage is finally at a manageable level, and the college funds we've set up for Kiera and Van are off to a healthy start. Quitting means moving back here and saying goodbye to all that because when we can't afford our mortgage and insurance and everything that comes with having kids, the first thing we'll have to do is dip into those savings. How can I focus on having a good life for me if it means my kids could struggle one day because of it? That might not be the reality, but it *is* a huge risk if I can't find something else. And I've tried. Since before Mack suggested the divorce, I've tried. The few roles I've applied for were highly competitive, and not many outside of New York pay what mine does.

I can't gamble with my kids' futures.

I'm their dad. It's my job to support them. To set them up in life. And I'm doing it.

It's hard to get the next words out, and my voice is weak when I manage it. "I want to know if Luke will be good to him."

Dad scratches his thinning hair. "Ah, yeah. I'd say so. He's fit in quickly around here. His friend though …" Dad shrugs.

"Thanks. That's all I need."

I finish off my tea, still ignoring the loud thoughts Mom is sending my way, and then I round up Kiera and Van. Van needs a change of clothes, but otherwise, they just need to wash their hands and hose their boots off before we're good to go again.

On the drive to the library, I keep glancing back at them. Van is staring out the window with his mouth hanging open, and Kiera is bouncing in her car seat and kicking the passenger chair in front of her. At three and five, they're at the easiest stage they've been so far, but that doesn't mean they're not hard work.

"Please don't do that."

She pauses and looks over at me. "What do you want Santa to bring you?"

Mack. Fuck, I'm an idiot. "Santa doesn't bring gifts for adults. Just kids."

"I don't want to grow up. That's not fair."

"Well … adults don't need toys. Santa makes toys."

"Then why did Harry Stevens ask for a PlayStation 5? A PlayStation isn't a toy."

"Ah …"

"Can we get a PlayStation 5?"

"No."

She doesn't look at all disappointed. "That's okay, I'll ask Santa."

Well, fuck. How do parents get out of this one?

I pull up in the parking lot behind the library, where Mack is already huddled on the back stoop. He's wearing a beanie, a scarf, and a heavy coat, and I'd bet he's got gloves on the hands buried in his pockets. I want to get out and hug him to warm him up, but instead, I turn up the heat on his side while he jogs closer and jumps inside.

"H-hey family!" he calls, sounding frozen but happy.

That's my Mack.

Always happy.

Always positive.

He makes my life that way too.

If he does start dating this Luke guy—or any guy—would that be taken from me? If he gets in a serious relationship, things will change. They'll need to. There's no way I could stay living in the same house they hang out in. There's no way we'll be able to have family movies cuddled up on the couch together. Or breakfast every morning when I'm home. Or … this.

Mack talking to the kids about how their day was and excitedly sharing his.

This will all become someone else's.

And I'm going to have to live with that.

"You okay?" he asks, all bright blue eyes and red flushed cheeks.

My smile comes easily because for right now, he's still mine. Kinda. "Yeah, I was just wondering whether to get takeout tonight."

"McDonald's!" Kiera yells, setting Van off into a chant of "Fries, fries, fries."

Mack palms his forehead. "You've done it now."

"Anything to keep my family happy."

6

Mack

"Thank you all for coming," Art says in a somber tone to the group around him. "It breaks my heart to say, but … Mack has gone to the other side."

Payne and Orson exchange looks, and I raise my hand.

"Ah, I'm right here?"

"Not *dying* other side. Relationship other side."

"Which is basically dying, as far as Art is concerned." Ford grins, squeezing Orson's thigh. They're sitting on the couch across from me in the top mezzanine at Killer Brew.

"I'll have you know my pookie has breathed fresh life into me." Art gives a flourish as he points at me. "But *you*. You were my last hope. My last look into freedom. If you're not single, who am I going to live vicariously through?"

"Your sister is single," Payne says, and Art's mouth drops.

"My sister? *My sister*? Mariana, the patron saint of abstinence? What is wrong with you?"

"She went on a date last night."

Art scowls. "I know. I had the niblings for her."

"Until what time?" I ask.

"What do you mean?"

"Well, did you have them until late … or all night?"

"It was a sleepover, but not because *she* was having a sleepover, okay? It was just easier."

"Uh-huh."

Art throws up his hands. "Here I am, trying to help my buddy out, and all I get is shade. *Shade*, damn you."

"Help me out?" I perk up at that. "What do you mean?"

"Well, my forlorn one, you're looking at the brain's trust. We, the great gays of the DMC—"

Orson raises his hand. "Bi."

"Ditto," Griff says.

Art scoffs. "Great gays and bis doesn't sound the same."

"What about …" I think. "Great gays and brilliant bis?"

Art tilts his head back to look at the ceiling. "Why? Honest question, *why*?"

"Hey, that works!"

"It's like a fucking tongue twister. The great gays and brilliant bis of the DMC."

"I think you originally had a point," Payne says. "That didn't involve alliteration."

"I give up. Mack is trying to win back Davey. Discuss."

My cheeks heat as my friends turn as one and stare me down.

"You want Davey back?" Keller, who's been quiet this whole time, asks. "We all knew you *wanted* him back, but you're actually going to do it?"

I hurry to nod. "He's home for *twelve weeks*."

"And?"

"*And* this is my chance."

Keller sighs, and I know he's about to hit me with logic.

I point at him. "No."

"But—"

"*No.*" I glare around at them all. "I'm done hearing about how I can't do it. About how it's stupid and nothing's changed. I don't care. I want Davey to realize we're the ones for him. That we're worth more than his job or the money or the travel."

"Yeah, but if you have to *make* someone realize that, is it worth it?" Keller asks.

"That doesn't sound very supportive."

Ford clears his throat. "One hundred percent support, but I have to say Keller makes a point. Luke's been asking about you a lot too. He's a great guy."

It's getting very hard not to be cranky. Why is it that I'm the only one who can see that Davey and I are meant for each other? "I'm happy for him. But I'm serious. If you can't be supportive, please go."

"This *is* what supportive looks like," Keller says. "Giving you a heavy dose of reality when you can't do it yourself. Making sure you're not blindly walking into shit. As long as you know all the facts, we'll be here to help, no matter what."

That warms me a little bit. "Good."

"Now, you *do* realize Davey isn't going to quit his job?"

"I know it's a long shot."

"Not a long shot," Keller says, leaning forward. "He won't."

"Uh-huh."

"And that you'll probably end up hurt."

"Very likely."

"And that we don't want to see that."

"You're a good friend."

Keller drags his fingers through his long black hair. "In that case, what do you need from us?"

"Ideas." I'm almost bouncing in my seat. "Ways to show him what he's missing when he's gone."

There are mixed looks around me, and it makes me snap.

"I said supportive, dammit!"

"A trip," Griff says. "When Fe was little, Poppy and I used to go camping for a weekend in the mountains. We'd switch off from everything and have three days together, swimming and exploring, going on hikes … it was great. You could do something like that."

I can see it now. Kiera and Van playing in the water … looking for lizards … me and Davey watching on. Sitting up later than them by the campfire … moving closer …

"It's perfect."

"What is?"

"A little trip together. It's right before Christmas, so it's not like Kiera's learning so much that missing one day of school won't be an issue." This is good. I pull out my phone to jot the idea down. "You guys are geniuses."

"Actually, the genius was all me," Griff points out.

"That's just one thing though," Ford says. "You can't expect one weekend away to do it all. You need a list. Now, not to toot our horns or anything, but you might be sitting in a room of the most romantic men in Kilborough."

"Minus Griff," Payne says.

"Hey! I had a very successful marriage. I think you mean Art."

"Can't mean me," Art says. "I pulled a fire alarm to have alone time with my man."

I scramble to open the notes section on my phone. "Fire … alarm …"

"Don't write that." Orson laughs as he tugs my phone off me and grabs a notepad and pen instead. "I'm sure we can come up with a list that doesn't involve misdemeanors."

Ford thinks. "Our love story started with a near drowning."

"Ours had a sword fight …" Payne adds.

"I was stabbed …" Griff muses.

Keller lifts his hands. "Don't look at me. I only *thought* about handcuffing Will to the bed for his own good."

Orson covers his mouth with both hands. "I'm very worried about all of your partners." He shoots a look at Ford. "Even yours."

My gaze pings from one friend to the next. "I would have thought handcuffing to the bed was a good thing. No?"

"Not in this case." Keller crosses his arms. "My best bit of advice is to find shared interests and spend time doing them. Will and I …" A smile trembles across his lips, and *urg*, I want to be that happy and in love again. "Let's just say that we've found a lot of ways to do that."

I huff. "We were only talking about this the other night, and other than the kids, we *have* no shared interests."

Art cocks his head. "None?"

"Nothing."

I don't like how the guys go silent. It sets off the doubts again that make me squirm.

"So. Dinners." Payne points at Orson to write it down. "It can be simple, but something you know he enjoys. Make it a bit special with candles or something."

"Okay." I drink the advice in.

"Flowers are always good," Ford says, patting Orson's thigh. "I know someone who can give you a family and friends discount too."

"Really?"

Orson smiles. "I'm sure we can work something out."

"Does Davey *like* flowers?" Griff asks.

"It's the thought that counts."

"It's true," Art agrees. "We can give you a whole list, but none of it will work unless you tailor it to you. People don't care about things; they care about moments."

Payne snickers, and Keller rubs at his temples, but that sounds like perfect advice to me. Tailor things to what Davey wants. But what are the types of things he likes? Work. That's all I can come up with.

And with that realization, it dawns on me that maybe this divorce wasn't completely his fault.

I bury my face in my hands. "Oh no."

"What's wrong?" Griff rubs my back.

"I'm a horrible person."

Again with the silence.

I groan and rub my fingers into my eyeballs, then look up again. "I think I'm the problem."

"You're going to have to spell that out," Orson says kindly.

"The reason we don't have anything in common. The reason I can't think of anything romantic. Hell, probably the reason we got divorced in the first place—"

"You *did* suggest it," Art points out, right before Keller belts him over the head with a cushion.

"No, he's right." I'm miserable as I sink back into the couch. "When I think of Davey, all I can think about is work. But that's not the man I fell in love with. It's just the biggest thing I started fixating on in the last year we were together." I stopped paying attention to him. Stopped making an effort. Instead, while Davey was working his ass off for our family, I was working my ass off to grow my resentment. I'd been happy in the delusion that *he's* the one who chose this divorce, but maybe it's not all on him?

"What does he do to relax?" Payne asks. "Beau colors in my tattoos, and that helps both of us."

"I have tattoos." Lots and lots of them. Down both arms and some on my torso. Maybe he could do that?

"You're missing the point. If coloring isn't something Davey enjoys, it'll be annoying for both of you."

Hmm … I twist my black wedding band round and round my pointer finger. There has to be something. "Oh. LEGO."

"LEGO?"

"He loves it. We had to build a shed out the back for him to keep his collection. He's always building things with Kiera and Van when he comes home."

"Okay …" Art glances around at the others. "Can any of you think of something romantic to do with LEGO?"

No answers. Well, fuck.

"Umm … he likes food?"

Orson jumps on that. "Then the dinners are a great idea. Cook something he loves and—"

"I hate cooking."

More silence. I want to kick something. This shouldn't be so hard. We're supposed to be together. We're soul mates. If two people are supposed to be, then shouldn't everything magically fall into place? Shouldn't there be signs pushing them together?

"What if I'm wrong?" I whisper.

Art's gaze sharpens on me. "No."

"But what if—"

"Nope. Support only, remember? We've already covered off the negatives; now we're all in this. If you're wrong, we're all wrong. And let me tell you, Artur de Almeida is never wrong."

"You had me right there with you until that last line." Payne sighs.

"Before Art got all humble on us," Keller says, turning to me. "He was right. We're not letting you quit. You know what you're getting into, you know the odds, and now you have every one of us behind you, helping you strengthen those odds. We all love Davey. We all love you. And I know I speak for all of us when I say you two belong together. We just have to figure out how to make it happen."

Orson's nodding, and Ford's smiling, and Griff gives my shoulder a squeeze. I'm stupidly close to tears as I realize how lucky I am to have these guys on my side. I throw my arms around Keller.

"Thank you!"

"Yeah, yeah …" He pats my back. "I only have one thing I want to negotiate on Davey's behalf."

"What is it?"

I pull back as Keller pins me with a look. "Nothing shady. We're here to help you reconnect with him to a point where you feel comfortable bringing up your relationship again. There's no tricks. No manipulation. Just you reminding him that you love him by putting in effort, and then you need to promise to *talk* to the man."

"I promise."

"Good." He rubs his hands together and looks around at the group. "Who's ready to get romantic as fuck?"

7

Davey

"We're going away together!" Mack announces at the table the next morning. "Next weekend. It's going to be great. Just the four of us."

Just the four of us? My chest swells at the thought. "Where are we going?"

"That's a surprise." His sweet blue eyes are twinkling in a way I haven't seen in a while. It makes me want to lean over the table and kiss him.

"A surprise?"

"Trust me: it will be fun. *Gah.* I can't wait."

I'm grinning as I get up and clear the table. I can't wait either. Whatever it is will be a fun time with my family, and I love seeing Mack this excited about getting to surprise us all.

"What are your plans for today?" I ask him as Van slurps

his milk from the bowl and somehow gets it all down his shirt and all over the chair.

"Need to run to the shops for a few things. I was going to take the kids to the park later, but it will depend on whether some of the frost melts."

I hold up both hands with my fingers crossed. "Looking good for a white Christmas."

"Urg, I hope not. Make the snow wait for as long as possible. It's cold enough as it is."

Maybe it's selfish of me to want that magic when Mack gets cold enough on a good day. I shrug and scoop up his and Kiera's plates.

"Ah, I mean …" He hurries after me. "It would be amazing. And I hope you get it. I'll, umm, stay inside. That's all."

"You don't have to want it because I do."

"Of course I do!"

I start at the way he shouts it, and judging by his horrified face, I'd say it caught him as much by surprise as me. I chuckle to break the weirdness. "It's okay. We're allowed to like different things."

Mack *hmphs* and throws himself onto a barstool.

"Everything okay?"

"Fine." He attacks his thumbnail with his teeth, giving me the very clear message he's *not* okay. But with his hand up like that, my gaze hovers on his wedding band. The fact he still wears it does strange things to me, even if it's not on his ring finger.

"Hey …" I'm nervous even suggesting this. "Why don't I call Mom and Dad and see if they want to spend time with the kids today? You've had a big week at work, and I know me being home changes the dynamic around here, so you can take the day to do … whatever." And hopefully, that whatever isn't calling Luke.

"Yeah … That might be good."

I know Mom and Dad won't care because they're usually busier during the week than weekends, and they want as much time with the kids as they can get. If not, I'll take them to the arcade or out for lunch. *Something.* I'm kind of hoping that with the kids out and me and Mack here alone that *we* can spend time together.

I'm not sure how to suggest it without *I'm still crazy in love with you and want every second I can get* falling out, so I zip it and call my parents instead.

Mom is overjoyed, and somehow, I manage the phone call, the drive over there, and then tea with them both without them reminding me that my husband is going to get away and I'm a giant idiot for letting him.

I feel like even more of an idiot when I get home and he's not there though. The house is echoey and silent, and given I was out with the car, that has to mean Mack got picked up by someone.

Luke?

I huff and dump my things in the kitchen before heading out to my back shed. It's the best place to distract myself because when I get too far into an intricate build, my whole brain goes silent. And silent is what I need.

I flick the light on, and the space instantly comes alive. It's less of a shed and more of my dreamland. We've plastered the walls and installed ultrawhite lighting, and every wall is lined with as much shelving as we could fit inside. Each shelf has mini spotlights, pointing at the sets I've finished and have on display, then right in the middle of the space is a huge five foot by five foot table with everything I need in organized drawers underneath.

This is what heaven looks like.

With all my travel and then having the kids most of the time while I'm home, I don't get to spend as much time in here as I'd like. Kiera's gotten to a good point where she can follow the instructions, but Van still has no idea. I have a bucket in the corner next to a bean bag where he can play with the giant blocks we've gotten him, but I'm always too on edge with the little tornado in here to actually concentrate on what I'm working on.

I make my way along the shelves, inspecting the sets, until I reach my pride and joy. The Millennium Falcon. It hasn't moved, and judging by its pristine condition, Mack really has been out here dusting it for me.

A wave of emotion sweeps over me that even without being here, even with us not being married, he's still looking after me.

That man is too good for words.

Maybe Luke does deserve him? Or if not Luke, someone else who can be here all the time for Mack to fuss over? Who'll appreciate everything that incredible man does.

"Hey …"

I jump at his voice and turn to find him sliding the door closed behind him.

"Thought you'd be out here," he says.

"Not a hard guess though."

He takes a minute to look around. "I love this room."

"Right." It makes me laugh. "You said LEGO is—and I quote—more painful to build than to step on."

"I didn't say I liked building it," he defends, crossing his arms. "It's peaceful out here."

"Thanks for looking after everything."

"Of course." He rounds the table to come closer. "What are you building?"

"Not sure yet." I duck down to look at the small sets I have sitting ready under the table for when I want to build something quickly.

Mack crouches next to me. "The car?"

"Hmm …" I shift it aside to see what else there is. None of it looks overly interesting. "You're back sooner than I thought," I say.

"Just had to duck to the shops. I said that."

"Yeah, but I had the car."

"I know. Ford picked me up. He said I could borrow Orson's car while you're back since they usually drive to and from work together anyway."

"That was nice of him."

Mack nods. "Ford's a nice guy."

"He is." The thought of him and Orson together still makes me laugh. "I have no clue where their relationship came from, but they work well together, don't they?"

"Yeah. They're happy."

"Total opposites though."

Mack snorts. "Like we can talk."

"Us?" I turn to him curiously. I've never considered me and Mack to be opposites at all. We're both family oriented; we both love Kilborough and our home here. We both prefer quiet nights in than partying, even when we first met. A lot of our values align, and sure, the superficial stuff—like his love of fantasy and my love of Sci-Fi—exists, but when it comes to the real things, we've always been on the same page.

Hell, even work.

It's not something we talk about a lot, but Mack works just as hard as I do, and his position is only part-time.

He's lucky enough to not need to travel for it though.

His sweet, pale blue eyes meet mine.

"We have a lot in common," I tell him.

He taps the box in front of him. "Like what? It's definitely not LEGO."

"No, but … the big things. The ones that count. We both believe in marriage. We both wanted kids. We're both kind to people and believe in second chances. We both put our friends first—" I catch the hollow meaning behind those words in a way Mack probably doesn't. Sure, I put my friends first, but did I do the same with my family? I'd like to think it's a yes, but walking away from Mack will be something I'm torn over for the rest of my life.

I steer the conversation back to safer ground. "So … next weekend. I think I can get it out of you."

His face lights up. "Nope. My lips are sealed."

"What if I guess? Will you say yes or no?"

"Hmm … maybe."

"That's not an answer."

"Of course it is. It means I'll answer unless you get it right, then I'll be all edgy about it."

"Edgy, huh?" I rub my stubble. "Let's see … that science museum in Springfield?"

"Nope!" His expression shifts. "Wait. I take it back. I just realized I can't answer at all, or it will be obvious."

The panic on his face is so cute I can't stop myself from laughing. Can't stop myself from touching him, even if it's only to give his arm a squeeze. He just makes me *happy*. "You're right. I'll let it go so you can have your surprise."

"Thank you."

"I'm excited though. No pressure."

"Suddenly feeling all the pressure."

We smile at each other for so long it makes me remember when it was always like this. My heart aches for it again, and I can picture how easily it would be for me to lean forward and kiss him. I remember exactly how those lips feel. Exactly how he tastes and the sounds he makes.

It's sweet, sweet torture to have had it all and lost it. And with no changes in my future, it would be unfair of me to act on any of it, even if I see that same longing staring right back at me.

I clear my throat. "Car one, it is."

I grab the box and stand, and Mack follows me stiffly a second later. Only he's too enthusiastic. He shoves to his feet, hip knocking the corner of the table, and when he jolts back a step, I try to steady him.

Wrong move.

Mack stumbles off-balance and falls back into my shelves, throwing out a hand to catch himself. The whole wall of sets sways concerningly, and while I'm watching my babies, prepared to catch any that fall, Mack's hand closes over the gun turret of my Millennium Falcon.

Instead of catching himself from falling, Mack crashes to the ground, and my spaceship flips and follows him.

I watch, like it's in slow motion, as the set that took me over a week to build hits the cement floor and explodes. Six thousand carefully constructed pieces shoot in every direction, and as the shattering and crashing goes silent, two smaller sets smash over the top of the mess.

The ringing in my ears that follows is deafening.

Mack's mouth is somewhere around his ankles.

"Holy … shit. Fuck. Davey, I'm so … so sorry. I didn't … I didn't mean …" His voice breaks, and I know I need to reassure him, know it wasn't his fault, but my voice has vacated me. I'm frozen.

My pride and fucking joy is a mess of mismatched pieces on the floor. I don't know if I have the energy to hunt down every tiny piece, then sort through the ones that don't belong. Where the hell did I even put the instructions?

"Fuck!" I knew it. I *knew* I should have glued it. Knew with Van around that I was tempting fate, but I'd wanted to carefully pull it apart when he was older and build it again with the two of them. My fingers get lost somewhere in my curls as my mind races at how the hell to fix this.

Then I spot Mack.

Close to tears.

Looking fucking horrified.

And it hits me: it's just fucking LEGO.

"Hey, it's okay," I say, reaching for him. It's a total fucking lie since I feel like my gut has fallen out through my ass, but I'm not going to let Mack know that. "An accident. It was only an accident."

That part is true. I might be dying over the biggest set I've ever built being ruined, but Mack didn't do it on purpose. In fact, he's been doing everything he could to look after it for me.

I can only imagine how he feels.

I help him to his feet, hating the horrified expression on his face.

"I'll … I'll fix it," I say. "It will be fine."

Mack hauls me into a hug. "I'm so fucking sorry."

He squeezes me against him, and I wrap my arms around

his waist, face pressed into his shoulder. Maybe it makes me a horrible person, but fuck. It's kind of hard to care about LEGO when Mack's holding me like this. My freak-out can come later.

Right now, being in his arms, I'd sacrifice twenty Millennium Falcons to have this again.

DMC GROUP CHAT

Mack: I'll be offline most of the weekend. We're going camping, yay!

Griff: When you say camping, tell me this is a euphemism for something?

Keller: What exactly would that be a euphemism for?

Art: Pitching tents.

Orson: That feels like a reach.

Payne: Maybe he's camping out in Davey's pants?

Orson: I don't think any of you know how a euphemism works.

Griff: I'm more concerned about the fact Mack hasn't answered.

Keller: There's no way he'd be really camping. It's winter!

Art: Have you met Mack?

Payne: Well, this is concerning.

8

Mack

The snowfall isn't a great sign. I glare at it as I struggle to stuff the camping equipment away in the back of the car. It's all brand-new since life in the wilderness isn't exactly high on Davey's and my to-do list, but that's okay. This is going to be great.

Though, the snow does mean there's unlikely to be any swimming … or lizards …

Fuck. Okay. Pivot.

Fire. We can do fire. And s'mores—everyone loves those. I scuff a hand over my short hair, ignoring the way my heart is beating rapidly. This is all okay, it's going to be fine. Not only do we need to have the type of magical weekend where Davey swallows his tongue over being reminded how much he loves us more than work, but I also really, *really* need to give him something to make him forget last week's LEGO incident.

I still can't believe that happened. It was the exact opposite of what I'm trying to do here, and even though Davey told me it was fine and we scooped up all the pieces together into a box, there was tension around his eyes that's only there when he's holding everything in.

I don't want him to hold everything in. I want him to be happy.

Davey crosses the snow-sprinkled yard, carrying Van while Kiera kicks at the white frost behind him.

"Are we, uh …" He catches sight of the tent. "Ready to go?"

"Sure are!" I up my grin a notch and scoop a squealing Kiera off the ground before rounding the car to buckle her in. This is going to be great. So great.

We get to the campsite, and I can feel Davey's stare burning into the side of my face. I'm sure it means nothing that we're the only ones here.

The trees are stripped of leaves, and snow is lumped between the struggling grass poking through. But it's already started melting, so I'm taking that as a good sign. Even Mother Nature is on my side.

About time someone was.

Our campsite is right on the water, which would have been a good thing in the summer but now feels way too exposed to the elements as I pull the car to a stop and look out at it. I'm wavering on the edge of taking us back home again when a picture of the four of us laughing around the fire as we cook s'mores flashes through my mind.

It's going to be perfect. We can do this.

Then I get the whiff of something nasty.

"Urg … *Van.*" Of course he couldn't have waited until we got all set up.

I glance over at Davey, who holds up his fist, and we rock, paper, scissors who's going to change it.

It's only when Davey loses and jumps out of the car that I remember I'm supposed to be making this weekend good for him and probably should have just dealt with the poop. Changing a stinky diaper does *not* set us off to a good start.

Okay. Tent. I can do that. The guy at the store said it's a super-easy one to put together, which is a relief because I've never done it before, and truthfully, I want Davey to be kind of impressed that I'm capable of these sorts of things. I don't just talk books and charm old ladies, thank you very much.

I unzip the bag it comes in and stand back to look at the overwhelming lump of canvas inside.

Right.

Tent.

We can do this.

I keep one eye on Kiera down by the water and pull everything out. It looks like more of the frame is already inside, so I follow the instructions step by step, and—holy fuck—it *was* easy. I'm mind-blown that the thing took almost no effort on my behalf.

Van goes tearing inside it as Davey comes over.

"Looks good."

"Only the best for my family," I say, throwing my arm around his shoulders.

His hand finds my back, and even through the layers of clothing, it's comforting.

"So … camping."

"Griff said they used to love it when Felix was little."

"Griff's behind this. Got it."

"Do you … is this okay?" I turn to look at Davey. His face is so close to mine I get this wash of nerves deep in my gut.

It's been so long since I've seen his face up close like this, and my memory revels in his dark freckles, his long eyelashes, the flecks of warm brown in his dark eyes.

He gets that amused, indulgent expression I love so much. "We'll make it work."

Almost as soon as he says that, there's a loud splash, and Kiera shrieks.

"Daddy!"

We race toward the water's edge, where she's slipped and landed on her butt in freezing cold water. Her coat is saturated, her boots are full, and her little teeth are knocking together as I hoist her up out of the water.

My sleeves are instantly soaked as I carry her back up to the car, starting to shiver myself.

"What were you doing?" I ask, trying to keep my voice even. I'm not going to yell at her for slipping, but *come on, Kiera*, we're trying to get Daddy back here.

"There was a p-pretty rock."

A pretty rock. A pretty fucking rock.

I bite down my frustration and grab her bag. "Next time, ask for help."

"S-sorry, Dad." Her big eyes fill with tears, and I'm obviously not doing a good enough job of hiding my emotions. Which hits me right in the heart.

"No, baby, it's okay." I wrap her in my arms, which doesn't help either of us when they're all wet too. "Shit, wait. Let's get changed, and *then* we'll hug."

She giggles. "You said shit."

Well, fuck. "That doesn't mean you get to say it."

The wind is fucking freezing and picking up as I lock us in the car with the heat up. Then I strip her off and pull on some warm clothes. We only brought one pair of gloves, so that was stupid on my part, and it takes a few minutes of cuddling before our hands are warm enough to venture back outside.

Davey and Van are throwing rocks into the water, and I haul Van back.

"Didn't we *just* go through this with Kiera?"

"I'm not going to let him slip," Davey sighs.

"Me throw it. Me throw rocks." Van struggles in my arms, and when he squirms his way out, he runs back to join Davey again. I watch as he grabs a fistful of dirty gravel and throws it into the water, which flicks up toward him.

"Sure. Teach our son to throw rocks. Wonderful."

Davey sends me an unimpressed look.

I remind myself to cool it. We can talk about that later. Everything is fine here.

"I'm going to set up our beds," I say. "Do *not* let Kiera get wet again. She's only got one more change of clothes."

"I got thi—" He turns toward me, and his smile slips off his face. "Umm … where's the tent?"

"What?" I spin around, and sure enough, the tent has disappeared.

Disappeared.

"It was *just* there!"

"It's fine. It can't have gone far," he reasons, passing me to go look.

I scramble after him, and we find the tent in a ditch on its side, tangled in a crop of what was bushes before they lost their leaves. One corner has dipped into the river and is taking on water.

"Oh no."

I shoot forward to grab it, and Davey helps me free the

stupid thing that is fucking stupid. The wind keeps trying to pick it up, and the damn tent is acting like a sail.

By the time we get it back to where it was, I'm starting to sweat, and Davey's curls are a wild mess.

"I think we're supposed to peg it," he says.

Of course we fucking are.

We find the pegs, and I have no fucking hammer to set them in, so we go around, one by one, trying to stomp them into the hard earth. My foot hurts, even with my heavy boots on, my undershirt is sticking to my back, Davey's dark face is flushed with exertion, and today is rapidly swirling away from me.

We need this tent up. Then I can get the bedding, and we'll read some books and play some games before we get started on the fire. It will be perfect.

Splash!

"Arg! Dadda!"

You've got to be fucking kidding me.

My eyes meet Davey's wide ones. There's a split second of what-the-fuck-have-we-done that passes between us before he shakes it off.

"I'll take this."

He goes to grab Van, and my head falls back toward the lumpy white sky. I can still save this. I can.

Only story time turns into Kiera and Van nonstop arguing over which book to read, and then Van keeps trying to join in our card game and scatters the Uno deck everywhere. Kiera gets angry that he isn't playing properly, and when I snap at her for throwing her cards, she bursts into tears.

Van follows, because why the fuck not, and I'm seconds away from following them too.

The headache building behind my eyes isn't helping matters.

"Fire. I'm making a fire." It's the only thing I can think of to salvage this. The body heat must have built up in the tent because it's fucking freezing outside. I zip my puffer jacket up my chest and duck my face into my scarf as I go in search of wood I can use. There's a fuckload of bare branches that will be perfect for this kind of thing, and I wonder if being cold will be a problem. I've never done this before, but I bought kindling and some matches, so I'm already one up on Bear Grylls.

YouTube is my friend, and it takes me half the box of matches before anything happens, but I finally get a small flame. Which goes out quickly.

"Fuck my life," I say, squeezing my eyes shut for a moment.

"Hey …" Davey's hand rests on my shoulder as he crouches beside me. "Everything okay?"

"Me? Yeah. Fine."

"You seem stressed."

"Stressed?" My voice jumps up a notch. "Look where we are. This is beautiful. And I'm with my amazing family. What on earth would I be stressed for?"

Davey smiles kindly at me as he takes the matches and gets the fire lit. "Kids are a lot."

"Why don't they appreciate this?" I huff.

"Who said they don't?"

I gesture dramatically back toward the tent. "All they've done is complain."

"They're little people with big emotions. Their bodies are too small to hold all that in, so it spills out. We're lucky to be the safe space where they can do that."

I flick a confused look toward him but can't handle this conversation right now. "Just … sucks."

"Why are we here, Mack?"

"Family weekend. We haven't done one of those in forever."

He presses his lips tighter, like he's trying not to smile. "But why, during winter, did you think *this* is where we should spend the weekend?"

So I didn't think it through—it's not like I need that pointed out to me. Instead of answering, I shout over my shoulder, "Who wants marshmallows?"

Kiera and Van immediately answer the *save me* cry and come tearing out to join us. The lingering look Davey gives me tells me this is far from over though.

After a burned lip, two burned fingers, Van's scraped palms, and a barely edible dinner, we climb into the tent for bed. The kids are out quickly, but I lie there, listening to the wind tossing things back and forth outside, with Kiera's foot in my face, and stare at the canvas overhead, dreading another day of this.

Davey's hand finds mine, and he gives it a light squeeze. I look over at where Van is sleeping over his neck.

"This … this was okay … right?" I whisper.

Davey's indulgent look is back. "I loved it."

I can't stop the scoff that leaves me. "That's an exaggeration."

"I'm with my family. You're right, we do need to do this more."

Something about the look on my face makes him laugh.

He squeezes my hand again, tighter this time. "But we can definitely go home in the morning."

"Oh, thank god," I groan, covering my eyes. As happy as I

am to not have to keep this going, it doesn't help that the only reason for that is I failed.

I'm an idiot.

If anything, I've probably pushed Davey further away from us than ever.

9

Davey

MACK'S IDEA WAS A GOOD ONE, BUT THE EXECUTION? FUCKING hell. When he gets excited about things, he jumps into them headfirst, which means we have a fifty-fifty shot at either a fun time or sheer fuckery.

The camping trip wasn't anywhere near as bad as he made it out, but that doesn't stop him from moping about it the whole way home.

In fact … I wasn't lying when I said I loved it. I'd left my phone in the car and just focused on being with them, picturing what it would be like if we were still married. That means embracing the good and the bad because if I hadn't been there for Van's tantrums, I also would have missed the way he clung to me all night. If I hadn't helped Kiera through the pain from her burns—which was totally on us—I wouldn't have gotten sunrise cuddles with her telling me about her friends at school while Mack and Van slept in.

I only wish he'd go easier on himself.

It's not until we pull into the driveway and I'm climbing out of the car that I hear him mutter, "Can't even manage the perfect stupid weekend."

Perfect weekend?

I close my door and take a second before reaching for Van.

Mack wanted the perfect weekend? But … why?

Is it because our time together is so limited? Because he wants our family together as much as I do? Or, more likely, does he know that with him dating, everything is going to change?

I'm not an idiot. Mack is a fucking catch; my parents don't have to keep reminding me. I'm shocked he's managed to stay single this long, but once he finds someone, he'll hold on to them. That's who he is.

And if there's another man in the picture, we won't have this anymore.

Weekends away with the kids? Snuggling in a tent? That all stops, and rightfully so. No matter how I feel about Mack, I'd never jeopardize another relationship for him.

Are these three months the last we'll have like this? I haven't seen Luke again since the morning he showed up, but that doesn't mean he isn't visiting Mack at work. If I know my husband—*ex*—like I do, he would have asked him not to stop by while I'm home. He's respectful like that, but it also means I can't keep an eye on the guy.

We bring the kids inside, leaving the rest of our things in the car, and I look around our living room, feeling a pang of love and regret.

None of the decorations are up yet because we normally do

it the week or two before Christmas when I'm home to do it with them.

But I'm home now.

And this might be our last chance, just the four of us, to make it special.

It's too late to manage a perfect weekend, but I can at least try to give Mack a perfect night.

I start a new chat and add Art, Keller, Orson, Payne, and Griff to it.

So, I hear Griff came up with the fantastic idea for Mack to take us camping.

Griff:

Summer. I thought he'd wait for summer. Or at least spring.

I laugh before I write back.

And since I'm assuming the rest of you supported this idea, you now owe me.

Payne:

Ever since I joined this group, I'm constantly being dragged into fuckery.

Art:

You're welcome. Now what do you need, Davey?

What do I need? I think through my plan and what the first step will be.

. . .

OKAY, FIRST, I NEED ONE OF YOU TO CALL MACK AND TAKE HIM to do something this afternoon. The rest of you are going to cancel your plans and come over here. We have crafting to do.

Art:

Goddamnit. I told Joey that having friends was a bad idea.

Orson:

We'll be there. Want to fill us in on your plans?

Me:

Apparently Mack wanted the perfect weekend and he feels like camping went to shit—not far off, honestly. So I thought tonight we'd put the Christmas tree up with the kids, but because Kiera and Van are monsters half of the time, that could be either family fun or complete chaos, so I want to skew the odds in our favor.

Payne:

I'm not helping you drug your kids.

DEAR GOD.

ART:

Why not? Bit of rum on my pacifier did me fine as a baby.

Keller:

Thank you for making Payne's point.

Me:

No drugging. Well, kind of. We're going to keep them busy with shiny ornaments, hot chocolate, and treats after a day of one of you wearing them out. Plus crafts. Lots and lots of crafts. I want this place to look incredible.

Art:

I don't like where this is going.

Me:

If you think I'm letting you and your dick brain anywhere near the crafts, you're mistaken. Uncle Art gets to do energetic stuff.

Art:

Since Joey makes me keep you fuckers around, he's definitely getting roped into this.

Orson:

I have an idea. And Ford will help.

RELIEF WASHES OVER ME AT HOW EASILY THEY'VE ALL JUMPED on board. Maybe they had plans, maybe they didn't; it doesn't matter because not one of them has questioned me or given pushback.

GRIFF:

Given my last advice went so horribly, I'll be the one to take Mack out. I'm suddenly agreeing that I might not be the romantic one of the group.

Art:

Thank you. My title has been restored.

I CLOSE OUT OF THE CHAT, THEN WAIT FOR THE MOMENT Mack's phone rings.

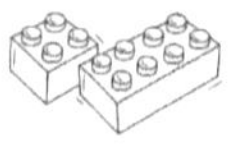

OKAY, OKAY, OKAY. I GIVE MYSELF A PEP TALK WHILE I WAIT for Mack to get home. I'm nervous as I pace the living room while Kiera and Van polish off their dinner. I've already dressed them in festive outfits, a decision I'm already regretting based on the pasta sauce covering Van's face.

But at least they're quiet.

And away from all the white.

I pace back toward the living room door and glance inside again. The tall pine is bare in the corner, with a giant box of decorations right next to it. The rest of the room? Well, it looks like a cloud threw up in there. Orson and Ford have covered the place in white roses while the kids, Payne, Keller, Art, and Joey all helped me make paper snowflakes to hang from the ceiling. Christmas carols are playing—thanks, Keller—and Payne lit a whole bunch of cinnamon candles that have been placed up well out of Van's reach.

Nighttime is pressing on the two large front windows, and I've dimmed the lights right down.

Now, all I need is Mack.

Fuck, I hope he likes this.

The soft sound of a motor lets me know someone has pulled up out the front, and I scramble to tidy up the mess the kids have made and clear their dinner from the table. Then I scrub at Van's face, pick the stray spaghetti off them both, and grab the tray of snacks I stashed in the fridge.

I've just set it on the living room table when the front door opens.

I can hear him in the hall, shuffling about, dumping his

keys in the bowl, and kicking off his boots. His coat will go next, then the scarf and his jacket. My whole body warms at the familiar motion.

Van goes to dart forward, but I hoist him up off the ground instead.

"Dadda."

"I know, buddy. He's coming now. Can you surprise Dad with a big smile?" He tries. "Bigger. *Biiigger.*" I tickle his ribs as a distraction, and he lets out the most adorable giggle—

Right as Mack steps into the room.

His droopy expression changes instantly to surprise as his big eyes move from me to the kids to the tree.

"Wha … what's all this?"

I put Van down and watch him launch himself at Mack.

"Daddy said we can decorate the tree." Kiera claps her hands together. "Can we start now?"

"Yeah, of course."

Kiera and Van run for the box of decorations and get to work while I approach where Mack is still standing.

"Why didn't you tell me? I could have helped you pick up the tree."

I shake my head. "If I told you, it wouldn't have been much of a surprise, would it?"

"You wanted to surprise me?"

Those big blue eyes meet mine, and the urge to touch him is almost overpowering. He still loves me. I know that, and I hope he knows that I still love him too. But sometimes love isn't enough.

I'm not selfish enough to say the words out loud, so I hope that showing him, making him a priority when I'm actually here to do it, is enough.

I gave him the divorce he wanted, but I never, ever stopped

loving him.

Not for a minute.

"You wanted the perfect weekend. You put in a lot of effort to make it happen, and I'm sorry you didn't enjoy camping. I wanted to find something to put that smile back on your face again."

The smile I love comes, and he hauls me into a hug. He grips me tight, face turned into my neck, and I press mine into his shoulder as I hold him back.

I fold as much emotion into the hug as I can, and it's torture. Torture to be this close but further from him than ever.

He lets go too soon, and I force myself to step back.

Mack isn't mine.

He's not mine.

My heart clenches as he turns to where the kids are setting up.

"Do I get to help?"

Kiera holds up an ornament she made at school. "This one."

He laughs and goes to join them, and I have to swallow around the lump building in my throat. These three are the reason I do everything. The reason I've built my life to be what it is.

So why do I suddenly feel like I'm looking in on a private family moment? One that I'm not part of?

"Don't think you're getting out of helping," Mack says, grinning at me over his shoulder.

I shake off the sudden melancholy and join them.

10

Mack

IT SMELLS LIKE A BAKERY IN HERE. A YUMMY, FATTY BAKERY full of food I want to put in my mouth. I can't stop looking around at our living room. I have no idea how Davey managed all of this in one afternoon, but Griff's sudden need for help with his back deck makes sense. Considering I'm not the most handy guy, I'd been so confused why he needed my help. And *outside*. It was fucking cold.

It was all worth it though. My body has thawed from the inside out, and if it took a disastrous camping trip to make this happen, I'll gladly live through that nightmare again. Our tree looks like the decorations have thrown up on it, and it's definitely more bottom heavy than anything, but I've never seen a better sight. Even when Van and Kiera get into a fight over a Santa ornament, Davey just scoops Kiera up to put the star on top, and the whole meltdown is avoided.

When they're almost finished, I lean back against the couch, legs stretched out in front of me and the tray of food by my side.

The feeling that settles over me isn't one I get a whole lot, so it takes me a moment to place it. Not confusion, not like I've taken a wrong turn. This is … I think I'm content. At peace.

Acknowledging that is enough to put a damper on it though. And I don't want that. I don't want the reminder this all has to end. I want to enjoy it and be grateful for these times, these moments, and hope we can stretch them out for a little bit longer.

Maybe when the kids are older, maybe I'll have to face the changes then, but for now, I'm going to sink into the *contentment* of having my family here with me.

Damn, my heart feels full.

It's a feeling I could fly on.

Once the tree is done, Davey makes us monster hot chocolates with whipped cream and marshmallows, then puts a Christmas movie on. I've already eaten too much sugar, but like hell am I going to say no to this. Kiera and Van kneel at the table while they drink as Davey settles on the couch and catches my eyes.

He pats the spot beside him.

I'm all jittery inside as I slide into the space. It's where I would have eventually sat anyway—once the kids were done and settled between us—but the fact he invited me here, just us, my gut tickles over it.

I clutch my mug with both hands so I have something to do with them.

"The Grinch? Really?"

"Kiera loves it," he whispers.

"It also gives her nightmares."

Davey's pretty dark lashes flutter with an eye roll. "That was one time."

"It might happen again."

He waves a hand toward the TV. "Feel free to tell her we're watching something else."

Yeah, I'm not dumb enough to do that. I hunch down on the couch some more, judging whether I can spread my legs wide enough that my knee will touch his. Given I'm still in jeans that don't like being parted, I'm worried I'll bust open the crotch before that could happen.

Dammit.

Okay, what else?

Even thinking about this is dangerous. The three of them, surrounded by all those flowers and snowflakes, really got me in the heart, and now I'm possibly going to be maybe ruining that, all because I want to touch Davey. Would he let me move closer? What about snuggle? It's not something we've done in years, and *definitely* not since we broke up, but men do that, right? When they're friends. Could we snuggle as two *friends*?

I shoot him a quick glance and find him already watching me. He catches his face in time because the soft look snaps into an easy smile before he turns back to the TV.

Something I need to do as well. The TV. The movie. We're watching it together, and I'm definitely not being distracted by my ex-husband and the insanely sweet thing that he did.

This is the sort of thing I should be planning.

Dammit, why is it that the one person who would kill it at planning sweet things for us to do is the one person I can't go to for help? Even I'm not dumb enough to be all *hey, babe, can you help me plan a date for us that I can use to get you back?*

Davey's knee drops against mine.

My gaze zeros in on the contact, wondering if he read that play from my own mind. He's wearing soft sweats—a pair of mine, I think?—which makes movement easier, and maybe I should excuse myself to go and get changed too.

Though now I'm more curious about excusing myself to go and see if that same pair of sweats is in my drawer. If Davey's wearing mine, I'll have no choice but to demand he removes them at once. Uh … after the kids are in bed. But then. *Then* he'd have to give them back. Immediately. While I stood there and watched.

"You okay?" he leans in to ask.

"Yup."

"Then why are you … are you panting?"

Ah. Fuck. I was breathing loudly. Not *panting*, but the thought of Davey taking his pants off is getting me hard. I really, really, really need to stop my mind from going there.

"Need to take a piss." I ditch my hot chocolate on the table and jog upstairs, hoping the exertion will get my cock to behave. He's my ex for a reason, and those reasons haven't changed.

But, fuck.

It's been years.

Maybe not for him, but I just can't bring myself to sleep with anyone else. As far as my dick is concerned, I'm still married, and the only guy it wants is Davey. I close my bedroom door and press my forehead to it.

This *isn't fair*.

Why can't I move on from him?

Okay.

Plan.

I straighten and glance over at my dresser. If my sweats are in there, I'll change into them and ignore the way I want to fuck him. I'll remember all the whys to the situation we've gotten ourselves into and forget the insanely sweet thing he did tonight.

If they're not in there … I don't think I'm strong enough to resist Davey wearing my clothes.

I flex my fists a couple of times, trying to convince myself this deal is stupid. If they're in there or not, it's not like I can just go and hit on my ex-husband.

We're in two totally different places. He's dated and slept around if his MyMatch profile is anything to go by, and I'm the forgotten ex who hasn't gotten the memo.

But daaaamn, it's been a long time. So long. If it was only one night, one hookup, would he be down for that? If he was getting it from me, *casually*, would he have to go out and find strange men while he's in town?

I'm sure he has his options in all the cities he visits, but Kilborough is a small place, and I don't want to be bumping into men who've sucked my husband's dick.

It's such a pretty dick.

The number of times we've been together is countless. I took it for granted, and where I could always count on another orgasm, now I struggle to even remember what he felt like against me, what he smelled like, how he sounded.

I crave it all again so much. The short visits home make these feelings manageable to resist, but it's already been two weeks of life with him, and it's not ending anytime soon. I'm *one* man, fighting for my life out here.

Fuck it.

With a decisiveness that doesn't come easily to me, I cross my room to the dresser and tug open the drawer. All of my pants are folded sort of neatly, and I have to sort through the stacks twice before I'm sure.

They're not here.

Those sweats he's wearing are mine.

Heat flushes my face as I strip out of my clothes and grab my thinnest, sluttiest pair of sweats. They won't keep me warm, but the kids will be asleep soon, and once that happens … I'm going to seduce my husband.

There's a soft knock at the door.

Fuck.

I scramble into the pants and tug a pajama shirt on, not bothering to button up the front before going to answer it.

Of course, it's Davey, leaning against the frame with his arms crossed and a smirk on his lips.

"I thought you were taking a piss."

"Wanted to get changed too."

"Right …" His gaze trails down my torso, and I need to remind my dick that it's nothing. Its time will come. "Just put Van to bed," he murmurs. "Kiera crashed out on the couch."

"That was fast."

"Eh. It's late, and Uncle Art wore them out today." Davey turns to go. "I'll put Kiera to bed, then we can watch—"

I reach out and pinch the waist of his pants. Davey pauses, glancing down before looking back up at me.

"What are you doing?"

Honestly, I'm on autopilot. I have no fucking clue. "These mine?"

"Oh. Yeah. You know I like—" He cuts off and shrugs. "It's never been a problem before."

"And it's not a problem now," I croak.

If I'd been holding out hope for him buying the same pair and mine being, I dunno, in the wash or something, that doubt is gone now. He's wearing my sweats. I made myself a deal.

Fuck, it's hard to get the words out. Almost impossible to

take that step. All I'd have to do is slip my thumb up, run it over his lower stomach, into that V I love so much.

But my hand is frozen, and I'm shitting myself with the thought.

"Mack …?"

"Yeah?"

"You need to let me go if I'm going to put Kiera to bed." His voice has deepened. This is my chance.

Kiera will be okay on the couch. If I let Davey go now, I might never get this courage again.

"You …" I'm debating what I'm going to say next until the words are already out. "You made tonight magical. You're always so good at that."

"It's nothing."

"It's not. I'm not the only one who feels it. There's a special sort of something in the air when you're here with us."

"Me?" Davey steps closer, shaking his head so those glossy black curls dance with the movement. "You've always been the one we center around. Just look at what you planned for us this weekend. I never would have thought of tonight if it wasn't for you."

"Except *my* plan crashed and burned." I sigh, still not letting go of him. "Sorry. That I couldn't make the weekend perfect."

"Perfect?" Davey steps closer again, and this time, his hands find my face. "My only perfect weekends are the ones with you."

11

Davey

I'M TREMBLING ON THE EDGE, LOOKING INTO THE SWEET BLUE eyes of the man I love, begging myself not to follow my instincts and kiss him. But he's here, and his face is so warm, and the way he's looking at me is taking me back to all those endless moments we've spent together.

I swallow roughly, thumb dusting over stubble, and Mack leans into the touch. Like he's starved for it.

My eyes mist, making the sight of him dip in and out of focus, and when he becomes clear again, his eyes are glassy too.

We're suspended in a moment that doesn't feel real, neither of us wanting to break the magic building around us.

His full lips part like he's about to say something, bottom one trembling.

"I love you so much," he whispers, and it kills me.

A stray tear finds my cheek, and I blink the rest of them away. "Mack …"

His hands cover mine, holding them to him, even as his expression turns from yearning to determined. "I know nothing has changed. Nothing. I think I love you more every day."

"Stop."

He steps in so our chests are touching.

I step back, but my hands are clamped in his, so I can't go far. "Don't do this."

He tugs me back closer, and this time, he releases one of my hands to wrap his around my back. "Please? I know what this is. I know that loving you won't change anything, and I'm not asking for you to give me anything more than one night. Just one. One where we shut the rest of the world out and ignore it until tomorrow."

My heart is aching to say yes. Every cell in my body is straining toward him, wanting Mack more in this moment than I've ever wanted anything. How can we both be so completely on the same side when it comes to our feelings but be on polar opposite ones when it comes to what we need from our relationship?

"I don't want to hurt you."

His forehead meets mine. "What if I want you to?"

"I can't."

"You can."

A soft, helpless laugh slips past my lips. "I'm not a strong man. Not when it comes to you."

"I don't want you to be strong. Not tonight. I just want you to be mine."

His lips ghost my chin, my jaw, creeping closer to the place they haven't been in years. My lips are tingling with expectation, breath hitched and shallow, waiting for Mack to do what I can't.

I slip my hands back, his short hair tickling my palms as I cradle his head, holding him close, breathing him in, stopping him from running away before he gets the courage we both need him to find.

His lips brush the corner of mine, and my heartbeat is so loud it's pounding in my ears.

I'm actually fucking nervous. Scared is something I was expecting; being close to tears makes sense as well.

But nervous? To kiss my own husband again. To touch him and hold him and, with any luck, to take him apart for the last time.

But maybe ...

I don't even let myself think it. Don't dare to hope that this could be getting us a step closer to where we both want to be. The only way we have a chance of anything else is if I walk away from a piece of who I am, but I'm scared without that piece that I won't have anything left to offer.

I suck in a shuddery breath as Mack's nose skims mine.

"Just one night ..." he whispers.

My grip on him tightens. "I ..."

"Do you still want me?"

That question makes me see red. "I've never fucking stopped."

I crush his mouth to mine, a rush passing through my body, so heady it almost knocks me off my feet. He's gripping me tight, pressing closer to my body like he's scared I'll disappear, and I'm clutching him back just as securely. I have no idea how many others have gotten to enjoy my husband, but I can guarantee they've never had him like this. Desperate and in love and afraid this will never happen again.

I know he feels it because I do too.

I hold his jaw, easing it open so my tongue can pass into his mouth. It's the deepest most indulgent kiss I've ever had, and my senses are in overdrive. The skim of his firm tongue against mine, his stubble scraping my mouth, his soft lips fighting to keep this going. Like he's begging me not to back away.

Now I've gotten a taste of him, that's impossible.

His body against me, his scent, his strong tongue, his hands gripping my shirt, all of it takes me back, and my memories hadn't done our time together justice. They never will. Because there's no possible way to capture how I feel with him, as though all my pieces have found their home.

Mack backs me toward the bed, and I go willingly, not breaking our kiss until he's pushed me backward onto the mattress. Our mattress. The place where we spent so many sleepless nights. Where we made love and found and held each other in the dark.

He covers me with his body, hard cock resting beside mine. But no matter how horny we both are for each other, I can sense Mack isn't in a hurry to get to that part, which is a relief because neither am I.

I'd kiss him forever if it meant staying like this.

It feels like hours with him lying between my legs, kisses deep and slow, hips rotating on a lazy rhythm that has me needy but not yet desperate. I want to bury myself in his body, watch his face as I bring him to pleasure, but there's a part of me that can't bear to face that moment. The painful action of putting on a condom to fuck my husband will break the moment we're escaping into.

I don't need confirmation of that.

So before he can think to ask, I roll Mack gently onto his

back and let my hand run over the front of him. With his shirt open, I get to explore every muscle, like a well-worn dream I want to sink into.

Then, I get to his sweats.

There's no hiding his erection. The pants do jack shit to stop me from feeling every ridge. He grunts into my mouth as I wrap my hand around him, and a shiver ripples down my back.

As much as I'd hoped for this moment, I never thought I'd get to make love to him again.

Sex with Mack has never been an issue, but I get the feeling this time is going to ruin me.

I pull back, breaking the kiss so I can watch his face as I reach for the band of his sweats and push them down. He does the same, large hands sliding the material over my ass and down my thighs until I can kick them to the foot of the bed. The head of my dick skims his balls, and my eyes roll back at the sensation.

This is happening.

Finally.

I'm going to lock this moment away in my memories forever.

I settle between Mack's thighs, and we let out matching exhales.

"You look so good there," he says. "You always have."

I manage a quick smile. "You know how much it turns me on to have you on your back."

He drags his nails down my back, my shirt dulling the pain until he reaches my ass. Then, he cups my cheeks and rocks his hips against me.

"Always so impatient."

"Only with you," he rasps.

As much as I want to sink into the compliment, it immediately brings up the question of *how many others*?

It immediately pisses me off. We're supposed to be blocking out the rest of the world and allowing ourselves this moment, but I can't bring myself to disconnect. There are a million thoughts spinning through my mind, questions around how I could let him go and how I can win him back and how many others has he been with?

I don't think he's sleeping with Luke, but if I hadn't come home early, would he have? Would it be Luke here instead of me?

The ache in my chest is painful, so instead of letting him see the battle I'm fighting, I bring our mouths together again. I try to burn this kiss into his mind. Try to remind him that no one will ever be as good for him as I am. It's not fair of me, but I can't help being selfish. I can't help bitterly wishing that Mack had never made me choose. I did everything, *everything* in my power to shower him and the kids with attention when I was home. I did *everything* to provide for them, I worked myself to the bone when I was home. But even giving everything wasn't enough.

I grind down against him, so keyed up and leaking that every thrust we share is mind-numbing bliss. Mack is bigger and thicker than I am, and his straight shaft fits so perfectly against my curved one it's like every aspect of us was made for each other.

The need in my gut turns static, balls aching with pressure every time they skim his. He lets go of my ass, legs locking around my waist and hands diving into my hair. We're sealed together in all the places that matter. Saying one last goodbye to the body I love so much. Our kissing turns fractured, panting breaths heavy and fast, mixing between us as I pick up the pace.

I'm hammering down against him, and Mack is chasing the high, hips canting to bring us together faster, harder, I rock toward my orgasm and know it won't be enough.

It'll never be enough.

His hand dives between us to lock around our cocks, and it's too much for me to fight anymore.

My dick swells with the incoming orgasm, balls tightening as the welling pleasure builds until I can't hold back.

Cum spills between us, and the gasp Mack lets out before he gently bites my bottom lip has me questioning whether it's just mine or ours. He keeps stroking, not letting up even when I get too sensitive for more, but I don't say anything. Neither does he.

We both hover there, stickiness building between our bodies as we work to catch our breath and extend our time together as long as possible.

His long, heavy exhale is like drawing a line between what we had and what comes next.

"Thank you," he says.

"Don't."

"I needed that."

"Yeah, well, so did I." I stop myself from telling him that I need *him*. Always have and always will.

With the orgasm subsiding, I'm thinking clearly again, clearly enough to know that the things we said, what we did, were all a stupid fucking idea.

It doesn't matter how much we want when there are things we can't get past. Sleeping together makes me want to ignore all those issues and fall back into our relationship, but it ended us once, and who's to say it won't be worse a second time around?

I need Mack in my life.

Even if it's only as my friend.

Doing this sort of mindless stuff puts everything we've worked for together at risk.

His voice is small when he speaks again. "This was a mistake, wasn't it?"

"If you're asking, you already know the answer."

I roll off him and onto the bed so he can sit up, and I try not to admire the way our cum looks smeared over his abs.

He drops his head into his hand. "I don't know what I was thinking."

I hurry to sit up too, moving so I'm next to him and can rest my forehead on his shoulder. "Sometimes the distance between us gets too much. We just needed to bring it in a little."

"Yeah. That's … yeah."

"Just because something is a mistake doesn't mean it wasn't necessary."

"I don't regret it," he says.

Even though it's a relief, it still hurts to hear that. I look up, finding him close, and can't resist brushing his lips with mine. "Me either. I'm glad it happened. And tomorrow, we'll find a way to move on."

12

Mack

Hey, universe? It would be great if I could stop making stupid choices. K, thanks.

When you question whether camping in winter is the dumbest part of your weekend, you know you're in real trouble.

I wasn't thinking beyond how much I fucking love that man, but even though I said I wouldn't regret it, I kind of do. Because now I fucking *hurt*.

Not regular-level hurt.

The kind of deep hurt that makes your soul exhausted. That comes with knowing the man you love loves you just as much, but the two of you are stuck in a stalemate, and there's no way forward.

A future without Davey doesn't seem like a future at all.

I torture myself, not for the first time, or the first hundredth time, with the question of why we aren't enough? He and the kids are everything to me. Why can't we be that for him?

I huff as I finish setting up one of the meeting rooms at work back to the standard layout. The knitting club likes to have a more relaxed feel in here for their weekly gossip, and unfortunately, their weekly gossip happened to include me.

Because Luke came in at lunchtime to see me.

Telling them, over and over, that he's just a friend was as useless as telling them the kids don't need any more scarves.

Part of the problem is me.

My heart is with Davey, but I know that I can't keep living that way. I know that I should be opening up my life to other experiences—especially since I'm now risking what happened last night to happen again—but how do I ask for that side of me back? Not only will it be the hardest words I've ever spoken, but it'll kill him.

It'd kill me even more if he agreed. If he moved out of our home. Stopped spending time together as a family. Stopped with the hugging and the movies and gaining energy by being in the same space as him.

Even though we're divorced, I've never felt like we're separated.

Davey isn't my ex-husband; he's the man I need to survive.

I sigh, leaning at the desk just as Tonya's walking past. She freezes in the doorway and glances back over her shoulder toward me.

"You okay?"

"Fine."

"Uh-huh." Her harsh black bob looks like a wig when she turns to me, and it sways as one. "Interesting that you're sighing so heavily after being visited today by a certain someone."

"Leave it alone," I say, warning in my tone.

She chews on her lip like she's debating whether to say anything, then throws her hands up in surrender. "Fine. How are the kids?"

My smile is automatic. "Amazing. They're loving having Daddy home. We put up the tree yesterday, and it was …" I don't have the words for how it felt to step foot into the living room, where Davey, Kiera, and Van were waiting, bright red Christmas shirts standing out against all the white. My heart flipped out all over the place, and it was a real effort not to cry.

But trying to explain to Tonya what he did and what it means to me won't work. Because there are too many details, and I'm worried I won't be able to hold back that we slept together. That nugget of information is all but bursting from me.

I might need to visit my friends and let it all out because otherwise I'm likely to blurt it to the damn knitting club, and then it'll be all over town by the time I clock out.

She hums, then carefully asks, "And how is the ex-husband settling back in? Sick of him yet?"

I scowl. "Never. The house doesn't feel right unless he's home."

"So … the winter festival is coming up in a few weeks …"

"Yeah, do you need help, or?"

"No, it's all organized. I was just going to point out that it's a magical night, and if you *wanted* to take a certain someone, I'd be happy to take Kiera and Van around for a few hours."

"Really?" My heart jumps at the thought of spending that time with Davey. It fits perfectly with my plan of reminding him how perfect home is.

I ignore the little voice telling me to let it go and beam at

Tonya instead. "You're an angel, you know that? I'll let Davey know."

She cocks her head. "Davey?"

"Yeah …" My excitement dims. "That we'll have a few hours to ourselves …"

"Oh." She tucks her hair behind her ears. "Only, I was sort of thinking it might be a nice *date* location."

"Exactly."

Her eyes almost jump from her head. "For you to go on. Romantically."

"Right."

Tonya face-palms. "Sure, yes, with Davey, sounds good."

I finally catch on to what she was implying. "Wait. With Luke?"

"Well, him or some other guy. It doesn't matter much to me. You're a catch, dude. You should be capitalizing on that."

My whole face goes hot. "No, I … I'm not ready."

"Will you ever be?" she asks kindly.

"I told you, I want Davey back. No one else."

She crosses to sit next to me. "And I'm supportive. I really am. I'm here for whatever will make you happy, but, like, I'm just saying … maybe it wouldn't be the worst thing to have a backup plan?"

"Why would I need one?"

"What's your ideal outcome?"

"That he quits work and is home full-time. Then we can be together again."

She's chewing on her lip again.

"Out with it."

Tonya can't look at me when she says, "That's not fair."

"What isn't?"

"Asking him again. You made him choose once, and he

did. What, you're going to back him into a corner and do it again? You're either going to make him feel terrible for having to choose his work again, or he chooses you, moves here, and then regrets it."

"He wouldn't regret it."

She lifts hard eyes, and each word is slow. "Mack. If that's the case, why didn't he do it the first time?"

"Because … because he …"

"Please don't do it. Nothing would make me happier than to see you and Davey together. You guys were couple goals, but if you force him into that place again, I don't see it going well. If he chooses you, it needs to be because he makes that decision."

I huff, that old resentment rising to the surface. "How could he do it? How could he put his job first? It's a job. We're his family. How, Tonya? I'll never get it."

"And that's your biggest problem."

"What is?"

"You don't get it." She gives me a sad smile. "It's not *just* a job to him. He's worked his ass off to get to where he is. He's put everything aside to get this promotion and make more time at home. If it wasn't for his job, where would you live? I know for a fact your salary doesn't cover that big, pretty house. What would you do with the kids if you had to work full-time hours? Would you even get those here, or would you need to find another job?" She looks resigned. "I hate that he didn't choose you. Truly. But I also don't think you're being fair to him. If he did what you wanted and left, moved home, your life would look a lot different. Would you guys have been in a place to get through that?" Tonya shrugs. "There's no way to know. But if you didn't, and things ended badly, and he'd walked away from the career he'd spent his whole life building, what would he have left? The kids are amazing, being a parent is a blessing —if you want that—but they can't be your whole life."

I scrub at my cheeks with both hands. "It sort of sounds like you're taking his side in all this."

She snorts and gives me a shove. "I'm always on your side, but every now and then, Mack, you need someone to pull that head of yours out of your ass. You're an idealist. You live in this golden world where everything is easy. Sorry to be the one to give you a dose of reality, but you needed it before you put your heart on the line again."

"Then what do you think I should do?"

"Keep being there for him. Keep hoping. Keep trying to remind him how much he loves you. But don't push. And just in case Davey does leave again, look at your options. Including one overenthusiastic cutie who has hearts in his eyes for you."

I thank her, and she leaves, dumping a whole load of thought on my mind. It's not weight I'd been prepared to carry around today, but as much as I hate having to shoulder it all, she brought up some very good points. Ones I hadn't thought of. I try to picture Davey here, in Kilborough, full-time. Every other time I've done this, all I see is coming home to happy faces, and the four of us at the dinner table and going to the park, and sitting up with him after the kids have fallen asleep.

That's what it's always been like. Those two weeks where he's home are perfection, so I've always assumed that would be normal for us.

If he's home more, would we fight more? Before I started getting resentful about him being gone, we never had any issues.

If he's here, would he find a job on the same income? Unlikely. It's a small town. It makes sense that I'd have to pick up more work to fill those gaps, and the library doesn't have room for that. I love this job, and the thought of leaving gives me that little bit of uncomfortable awareness of what Davey went through. Probably still goes through.

Kiera and Van would be in school more. Or with Davey's parents. That means a lot less time with their dads. I know that's how a lot of families have to manage things, but it's always been a point of pride that I'm there for every big and small moment the two of them have. If it wasn't for Davey missing Van's first steps, would it have been me? Both of us?

I've always held a slight chip of irritation that he wasn't there.

How would I have felt if I wasn't?

Devastated. That's how.

Fuck, is that how Davey feels about missing it?

I'm irritable as I reach the front desk, not liking this blinding look in the mirror.

It takes me a couple of seconds to notice the copy of *The Hobbit* sitting there.

There's no way …

I pick it up, and sure enough, there's a note poking out of the top.

Luke was here earlier, so it makes sense that he left another one, but I didn't notice it after he'd gone. So he snuck back and hid it, just so I'd find it on my own.

I stare at the slip of paper, not sure I want to touch it.

My realizations about Davey are blinding, and I don't have the mental space for anything else. But Tonya did say that it's worth having a backup plan.

And I do like Luke.

It's hard not to view this as a sign.

With a huge inhale, I tug out the paper.

Why don't you ask a Hobbit for money?

They're always short.

I grin at the joke and keep reading.

Sorry for the stupid jokes, I just like to see you smile. You're impossible to look away from when you're happy.

I blink at the words, smile sinking from my face.

All I want is a sweet man who'll love me like I love them. I want that man to be Davey.

But …

I read through the note again, then slip it into my drawer.

Maybe it's time to start being smart.

Maybe I'm putting too much pressure on Davey to fix everything for me when I'm the only one who can do that.

13

Davey

"Do you really need my help?" I ask Art, trailing after him into town hall.

"Yes. You're the only one not at work, so get your butt up here."

"You know, some people take vacation leave to … have a vacation. From working."

My friend pins me with his intimidating gaze. "You telling me you want to sit on the couch binge-watching shows all day?"

"I'd like to have the option."

He laughs and pushes open another door. "Such a liar. You're like me, and between the two of us, we wouldn't know what a day off looked like if it pole danced naked in front of us."

I think of Mack pole dancing naked. Fuck. "No, but I'd be interested enough to find out."

He gives me one of those looks that could be checking me out if I didn't know him better. No, this look is all assessing. Sizing me up. Which means there's something on his mind.

"How was the other night?" he asks.

The best and worst night of my last year. I don't mean for my sigh to slip out, but of course, Art latches on to it.

"That good, huh?"

And even though he's being a smart-ass, I agree. "Yeah. It worked perfectly."

"Then why the long face?"

Well, I can't tell him we slept together, so what other reason could I possibly come up with other than this sucks and it's hard and I want my Mack back? Another sigh balloons in my chest over my situation, but I smother it aggressively.

"Remember when you were all stupid eyes and falling for Joey?"

"Never happened."

"Yeah. Right. You definitely didn't stalk him at work or anything."

"I'm glad we agree."

My laugh is soft and short, just enough to release this tension. "Well, remember that feeling, and then picture having it every day from the second you wake up to the second you fall asleep."

Art slows his footsteps, and we hover in the hall outside of where the festival planning is taking place. "Have you given more thought to my suggestion?"

"Yes, and I appreciate you offering me somewhere to live." It means more than he knows. "I ..."

"Want to continue torturing yourself." He nods. "Got it."

Art stuffs his hands in the pockets of the expensive dress pants he's wearing. "You're both my friends. I give you both my opinion on what I think is best for your own scenario, not taking the other into account. You know I won't tell Mack that I've offered you somewhere rent-free for the weeks you're home, but I still think it's the best choice."

"I'd miss the kids too much." And Mack. I'd miss him too much too. Plus, there's that dark little fear that if I left, Mack would find it easier to move on. He'd forget about me, and all the Lukes in Kilborough could show up for him whenever he wanted.

None of those thoughts are ones I'll be sharing with Art. I trust that he doesn't share our conversations around, even though he has a reputation for being a loudmouth—under that playboy persona, he's a great friend.

"Also, I don't think I ever thanked you for offering to blow my husband." I narrow a glare his way, and Art cracks up laughing.

"I wondered if he'd tell you. He missed his chance now I'm locked down, but what did you expect me to do? A man should *not* go that long without getting laid. It's unnatural. Not to mention you've probably slept with whoever you wanted— he had to get the first orgasm out of the way."

Art goes to keep walking like he hasn't dropped a huge bomb on my head.

"Wait." I grab his arm and yank him to a stop. "What do you mean?"

"Ah …" His gaze flicks from me to the door and back again. "I don't mean anything. I laughed, and then I said nothing. Not a thing."

"Mack hasn't slept with anyone?"

Art's expression hardens. "You didn't hear it from me.

Don't look into it. This was months ago, and I have no idea if that's still the case."

Something in his face twitches, making me suspicious. "You're lying."

"Am not."

"What aren't you telling me?"

Both of his hands land on my shoulders. "You and your ex-husband are both pains in my ass. That's what. Now we're late, and you know how I am about punctuality."

He turns and strides toward the room before I can grab him.

"There was no arrival time," I call, but it's too late.

I know I need to follow him, know I need to go in there and help like I said I would, but my gut is breaking out in that wriggly nervous thing it does, and it's an impossible mission to forget what Art said.

Mack hasn't slept with anyone either. Or at least, he hadn't.

Is it still true? Has it felt as wrong for him as it feels for me?

I grit my teeth, wishing these were questions I could ask him. But what's the point? It's opening old wounds up for the both of us, and we're going through enough. Things have been normal, but … not exactly strained or awkward, just different. It's like every time I catch him looking at me, we're back at that night together, and I'm aching to kiss him again. I can already see it, how easy it would be to fall back into sleeping together. To forget about the worries we had and delude ourselves into thinking it will be different this time.

I don't trust Mack to be strong, so I'm going to have to do the work for both of us. Which starts with forgetting what Art let slip, helping with this festival planning, and not climbing Mack like a tree the second I'm home.

We get into it, and I offer suggestions for how to better manage the volunteer schedules. They've also got stalls set up way too far from the entrance/exit, which logistically would be the best place for them. I know that after taking Kiera and Van around, they'll be hungry and tired, so having that option on the way to the car would be a godsend.

"Look at you," Art teases. "A regular little event planner."

"God no," I shake my head quickly. "But when it comes to knowing what people want and how to market something, I'm your guy."

Art hesitates over the list he's working on. "So … that sounds like the type of job that would come with a high consultant fee."

"I don't hire out my services, but I know a few people who do, and they make a pretty penny."

He clears his throat and drags his pen down the margin of the paper. "Could do it from anywhere, I'd imagine."

Ah. What he's hinting at sinks in. "Technically, yes. The problem is if I was to take on consultancy for businesses, I'd still need to travel to them. Promotion isn't just about typing up a plan and handing it off to execute."

He drums his fingers on the desk, still thinking, and I cover his hand with mine.

"Trust me, I've thought about this. You don't think I'd move home permanently? When Mack first asked for a divorce, I spent the rest of the month trying to find something here that would fit. I was open to anything with similar skills and was even ready to take a slight salary cut, but while this place is getting bigger, it's still a small town. The opportunities aren't here."

"It kills me, you know," he finally says.

"What does?"

"How two people so perfect for each other and so in love can't find a way to make it work."

"Yeah. You and me both."

I'm distracted for the rest of the hour we're there, wanting to forget the way Art assumed it would be so easy for me to start consulting. Building that type of portfolio takes work, and while, yeah, working for myself would mean setting my own hours, there's only so much I can do from the home office.

Where I'm at now, I know these guys. I know how the company is set up and what each person's strengths and weaknesses are. I know the projects we'll be implementing soon and have a whole list of suppliers that keep our clients' costs down because of the regular work we supply. Doing that on my own? Not being there to manage the project?

It's not that simple.

I came to terms with that realization around the time I signed the divorce papers, but every now and then, I have a tiny flicker of hope that it could be different now. That something might miraculously turn up, but it never does.

The longer I'm home though, the more I remember I miss it. When I'm not here, it's like this deep-seated part of me goes cold and hollow, and no matter how much I'm enjoying myself with work and my colleagues, it doesn't ever go away. Not until I'm back. If I hadn't negotiated all this time at home, I'd likely already be gone again. The thought of saying goodbye to Van and Kiera again so soon makes me want to throw something. I know Mack thinks I'm the villain in all this, I know he thinks I broke up our family for nothing, but I'm fucking stuck, and I don't have a single soul to talk about it with. We have shared friends, my parents are on his side, and Mack, the one person I want to talk to more than anyone, is biased. His solution would be to quit and work it out.

Like it's so easy.

But what if I can find a way?

Urg, there's that hope again.

No matter how much I squash it down, it bobs determinedly back to the surface. And I think it always will while Mack loves me.

So I have two choices if I can't keep us continuing the way we are.

I either give him up completely, take Art's offer for a place to stay, and then encourage him to start dating.

Or I go back to figuring out the solution to our problems. And this time, I can't stop until I find it.

14

Mack

I'M QUICK AS A NINJA AS I CREEP INTO DAVEY'S LEGO HUT and find the container we packed all the pieces into the other day. Do I like LEGO? No. Am I any good at it? Also, no. Which is why I'm enlisting the group to help me the hell out.

The look of horror on his face is something I keep replaying, and the way he comforted me after just goes to show what a perfect-hearted man he is. I'm getting him a Christmas present too, but I figure with how busy we'll both be in the lead-up to the holidays, especially with him still getting work done from home, he's not going to get a chance to rebuild this —so I'll do it for him.

Well, me *and* whichever friends I can bug to help.

The last thing I want is for Davey to leave for work again only remembering the kids' meltdowns, me destroying his things, and a hookup I'm worried he regrets. At this stage, I'm doing everything I can to cling to our closeness, to make sure nothing changes from this comforting love we have for each other.

Could I be content having this for the rest of my life? No relationship, no sex, just Davey and his cute freckles and sexy curls and the way he holds my eyes when he smiles.

I'm still stuffing the Luke question down in my brain, wanting to ignore it as long as possible. He came by again for lunch, and again, I couldn't bring myself to say anything. The thing is, when I chat with Luke, he's so nice. A genuinely happy person. And while I'm sure he has some kind of crush on me, I'm not convinced he's looking for more than a friend by the talks we've had.

If that's all he's after and I bring up more, that could go downhill fast. And I like the idea of having him as a friend.

The LEGO rattles in the container as I walk out to the car. Art picked Davey up, and Kiera is at school. Van's with his grandparents at kindy gym. So now is the perfect chance for me to sneak away and get this organized.

I have to hope that Davey doesn't notice the LEGO missing before I can rebuild it and get it back to him. Given that he hasn't had a chance to get out there all week, I should be in the clear.

Instead of heading for Killer Brew, where we all meet up regularly, I drive out to Ford's Garage. It's a huge space, and I'm sure he can find a teeny corner to allocate to me and my plans. Plus, there's no chance Davey would stumble across it here.

Ford's in the huge garage when I show up, coveralls stained with oil, and when he catches sight of my car, he grabs a rag to wipe off his hands and crosses the gravel front lot to meet me.

"This is new," he says. "Come to take me to lunch, pumpkin?"

I climb out and round the car to the passenger door. "I'll take you to lunch if you help me out with something."

"What's that?"

I pull out the container and rattle it his way.

"Oh, no. No, no, no. That stuff is the devil."

"I know," I say desperately. "That's why I need help!"

Ford backs up, dirty hands raised in front of him. "I'll buy my own lunch."

Taylor comes our way, eyeing my box in confusion. "What's going on?"

"I'm asking the handiest man I know to help me with a project."

"Griff is the handiest man you know," Ford says. "I'm an idiot. Very dumb. My fingers are way too big for those itty bitty pieces."

"Ignore him," Taylor says. "This looks fun. What is it?"

"Some *Star Wars* ship thingie."

Taylor grabs the box and lifts it to see through the clear plastic. "As long as it's not the Millennium Falcon or anything, I don't see why we can't help."

Uh-oh. That sounds familiar. "Uh … out of curiosity, if it was, that would be … bad?"

"Yeah." They lift their eyebrows. "It's big and tricky and will probably take weeks if we're not working on it constantly."

"Right …"

Their curious stare settles into a blank look. "It's the Millennium Falcon, isn't it?"

I pull the folded-over instructions from my back pocket. "Little bit."

They take the chunky booklet from me, resigned. "I'll find somewhere safe we can work on it."

"Wait, what?" Ford yells after Taylor's retreating back. "But I said no!"

They wave him off and keep walking, and it's a real struggle not to smile over the fact I won.

"Stop it," Ford grumbles.

"Have I mentioned before that I really love Taylor?"

Ford rolls his eyes and stalks back toward his garage, with me following after him. No sudden movements and no smug jokes, and I should be fine.

There's a small group gathered around one of the workstations in the back, where Taylor is clearing tools and parts off a bench.

"Hey, hey, we're not on break," Ford calls, but his tone tells me he knows he's lost them.

"… always wanted one of these," one of the men is saying.

"When do you need this done by?" Taylor asks me.

"Ideally? Before Christmas. I sort of have a plan for it."

"Hmm …" They study the booklet, gaze darting from the instructions to the container of pieces. "And they're all in here?"

"Yeah, uh, plus two other … things. It all got smashed and mixed up together."

"That's going to make it harder."

"I know."

A voice comes from behind me. "This is interesting."

"Argh." I startle at Orson popping up to look over my shoulder. "Where did you come from?"

"Lunch break. Normally I catch Ford fucking around at this time, but he's not usually joined by the whole garage."

I sigh and point to Taylor. "I broke Davey's most prized

LEGO set, so I wanted to sneakily fix it for him. Only, it's all in pieces, and there are other sets mixed in with it."

Orson pulls a face. "Looks like lunch is canceled, babe."

"What?" Ford's face falls. "Did I get dumped *twice* for LEGO?"

"Technically, you dumped me," I point out.

Orson waves a hand. "At any rate, this is important. True love is at stake." Orson holds his hand out for the instructions and studies them for a second. "I think we're safe to get rid of all the red, pink, and yellow pieces. Then, we'll need to work off the list of included parts to figure out what else we need." He claps Ford's shoulder. "It's almost like building a motor. You'll be great at this."

"But … but …" He holds his hands up again. "My fingers. They're too big."

"In that case, I guess you won't mind picking up lunch? Some sandwiches will do."

Ford throws me an unimpressed look but doesn't argue.

Half of the guys standing around jump into sorting through the pieces with Taylor while Orson pulls me back from the group.

"I heard camping was rough."

"You could say that."

"Oh, we did. Many times, and I have the texts to prove it."

I gnaw on my lip, wanting to defend myself, but it really wasn't my best moment.

"Now that's done with, I assume you have another plan. Maybe involving all this?"

"The thing is …" I stuff my hands in my pockets and scuff my boot on the cement floor. "I'm already feeling lost."

"About?"

"Whether I should even be doing this."

"What happened to doubts not being allowed and that everyone just needed to say yes because this was happening?"

I lower my voice. "We, uh, hooked up. The night we finished decorating."

Orson's understandably shocked. "I think my flowers are at a one hundred percent strike rate."

"Don't want to know what that means. But it happened, and I keep wanting it to happen again, even though I know how stupid it is. We haven't fixed anything. We're …"

"Digging your hole deeper?"

"Right."

Orson crosses his arms. "But you still love him?"

"So much."

"Obviously the travel thing got too much for you, but if that was me and Ford, there's nothing that would get in the way of me being with him. I'd rather two weeks out of the month than no weeks out of the month. If you love someone, you make it work. You figure out what you can sacrifice and what you can't, and then you go from there."

I huff, frustrated. "That's the exact opposite of the advice everyone else is giving me."

"It's pretty fucking clear. If you love him, and you hate that he's away from you guys so much—go with him."

"With … him?"

"Sure, why not?"

Why not? There are a million reasons why, and they're all ones I've faced time and time again whenever I considered this question. "The kids have school."

"Then homeschool them."

"And my job—"

"If they can't be flexible, quit. You don't need the money."

"But … where would we live?"

"Wherever Davey does now. Next?"

I had plenty of reasons before we started this conversation that I'm scrambling to come up with now. "It's not a stable life for the kids."

"Kids are adaptable."

I shoot him an unimpressed look. "Stop making this sound easy."

"I'm not. Look, I get it's a hard choice. I'm only pointing out that if being together is the most important thing to you, you can make it work."

"And if not, I should walk away."

Orson shrugs. "Well, I wasn't going to say it." He gestures toward the LEGO. "What's the plan?"

"His gran used to host dinner on Christmas Eve and cooked the same meal with pudding every year. He used to love it, and we haven't had it for a while, so I thought I could learn how to make it and then give him back what I broke. Like, it's nothing special, but I thought the gesture—"

"It's perfect."

I perk up. "It is?"

Orson's expression sobers. "Thinking about people and making them feel special is the most important thing you can do. And I don't want to get all heavy on you, but speaking from experience ... I know what it's like to lose the person I love. I'm incredibly lucky to have a second chance at this, and because of my perspective, there isn't a single thing I wouldn't do to make us work. It's easy to let our issues get to the point we can't see anything else, but ... in the end, none of that matters."

Orson has a perspective no one else I know does. Losing his wife drove home how short life is, and the thought of losing Davey that way has me so fucking panicky I can barely breathe. On this side of it, with our marriage a distant memory, it's easy enough to think I could handle his traveling, but then I think of how it felt last time he left—when we weren't even together—and that confidence shrivels.

Am I being too selfish in wanting it all or nothing?

I don't like that I automatically know the answer to that question.

But both ways I look at it, waiting for him or traveling with him, have a distinctly difficult future ahead.

Finding someone else would be the easy option.

Too bad there's no one like Davey.

DMC GROUP CHAT

Art: Christmas Party! Ho, ho, ho, motherfuckers!

Keller: Are you already into the eggnog? And did you save some for us?

Art: Can confirm mild tipsy, much eggnog.

Payne: You drank much eggnog, or there's much left over?

Mack: Save some for me! I need a good night out.

Payne: Better not go to Art's party then, bu-dum-ch.

Art: Did someone say something about bums?

Orson: Literally no one.

Mack: I miss Davey's bum.

Art: So many bums! I'm crying. We're all in the festive spirit!

Payne: I'm scared to ask what bums have to do with Christmas.

Keller: Couldn't help yourself though, huh?

Art: Gather rounde ye numpties. There once was a songe called Little Drummer Boye, and people from all across ye lande sangeth of his bume.

Orson: I could be wrong (I'm not) but aren't the lyrics "pa-rum-pum-pum-pum?"

Art: No, they're "his bum bum bum buuuuum!"

Keller: And you'll be singing this for us tonight, correct?

15

Davey

"SHIT, NO, VAN!" I CHASE THE LITTLE MONSTER THROUGH THE house. He's done the dash from the shower, and his naked little body is sending water everywhere.

I throw the towel his way and miss, making him squeal and dart into the kitchen.

"Watch it! I almost dropped a pan on your head," I hear Mack shriek.

Already exhausted, I scoop up the towel and hurry to hunt Van down.

I find him crouching under the dining room table, his constant giggles giving him away.

"Not cool."

"Daddy, rawr at me."

"I didn't roar at you."

He cackles and goes to bolt, but I nab him just in time, and then I wrap him in the towel like a straitjacket and haul him over my shoulder.

"That's one contained," I cry out to Mack. "Where's the other one?"

"She was picking out toys to take with her tonight."

I make a mental note to remind her to pack clothes as well this time. Last time I dropped them off at my parents' for the night, I got a call an hour later, asking where their pajamas were. Apparently, five-year-olds can't be trusted with that level of responsibility.

I dress Van, then check both of their backpacks have everything they need before I let them pile toys on top. Then, I join Mack in the kitchen. The urge to wrap my arm around his waist and kiss his head is strong, but I remind myself that isn't us anymore.

"Smells good."

"Thanks, it's a vegetable casserole."

Which translates to a sloppy, saucy mess, but I'll eat every damn scrap on my plate. "Yum. But you know, you don't have to cook every night. I'm okay to whip up dinner too."

"I know," he mutters, face falling. "I … it's fine. I like it."

That's the biggest lie I've ever heard. Not that he hates cooking or anything, but I know there's no passion there. Still, every time I try to step in, he gently nudges me back out again.

Considering cooking isn't my thing either, I'm not going to fight him over it.

"I'll set the table."

It's another family dinner with Kiera getting food everywhere and needing to be changed, while Van is up and down constantly, either climbing around under the table or running from room to room, grabbing trucks and cars and action figures.

Somehow, we manage to get his plate cleared between us both, but by the time we're done, we're running late.

"What time were we supposed to be getting to this party?" I ask Mack.

"Seven. But if we're half an hour late, who cares?"

"Pretty sure Art will."

Mack pulls an *oopsie* face as he closes the front door behind us all. "Should I text him, do you think?"

"Nah. He'll enjoy his moment of being dramatic about it, and then we can all move on. It'll be like our early Christmas gift to him."

"Wait. Are we supposed to get them gifts?"

I laugh and sling my free arm around Mack's shoulders, then give in to that urge to kiss the side of his head. "It was a secret Santa, and I've got you covered."

The tension in his body relaxes. "Thank you."

"You can thank me by putting that one in the car." I nod back to where Van is stomping in the sludgy front yard. Still no snow, but we've been getting promising little fluff that melts instantly and makes the ground all wet.

"That's fair." Mack rounds him up while I dump the bags in the back and strap Kiera in.

Art's Christmas party is one of his more low-key gatherings. This one is our friendship group, plus a few friends of friends, instead of the entire Divorced Men's Club, and he always does it early in December to stop it clashing with the festival and any other family things people have on.

It usually ends up getting messy, hence why the kiddies are off for a sleepover. Not that I plan on drinking a whole lot, but I know Mack will. Which is fine by me. My husband is an adorable drunk, which isn't a thing many people can pull off.

Mom hugs me and Mack tight when we get there, and the

kids rush off to show Dad the hoard they've brought. I'm about to follow them when my phone rings.

The name on the display makes my gut sink.

"Ah, I need to take this," I tell Mom and Mack before stepping into the front bedroom. "Hey, Eric, what's up?"

"Davey, how are you? How's the family?"

Fucking torture. Not that I can say that. "Everyone's good. I gave them a nice surprise by being home so early."

He chuckles. "I bet you did. This job has put a strain on you all, I know that, but the kids must love having Daddy home."

"They do. I don't think Van has slept a full night in his bed since I've been here." It slices my heart the way he climbs into my bed and wriggles after me in his sleep all night.

"Blink and you'll miss it age, huh?"

"Exactly."

Eric takes a deep breath, immediately pinging my suspicions. "Look, I love that you're getting that time with them. You've worked hard, and you deserve it."

"But …"

"Something's come up."

He doesn't have to say more than that for my gut to drop through my ass. "What is it?"

"Don't worry, you get the holidays with your family. I'd never get in the way of that."

"Then …"

"We've gotten a new contract. *Huge* client. Near unlimited budget." His tone turns regretful. "I need you on this one, and it's a tight turnaround. Issues with their last PR company."

My mouth has dried up. "When?"

"January second."

I can't speak. That's over a month earlier than I was

supposed to be leaving again. They'd promised me I could get my work done from home, given me hope that I'd be able to leverage more of that opportunity in the future. Hopefully do a good enough job to make it a permanent arrangement.

I awkwardly clear my throat. "You gave me twelve weeks here."

"I know. And I hate that I'm even asking, but we're desperate."

"Why can't someone else do it?" My voice starts to rise, and I smother it again. "Anyone on my team. Surely there's someone who can take this on. Come on, Eric, that only gives me three more weeks here." The rapid beating of my heart is sending my panic on edge. He can't do this—well, he can, but surely he *won't*. I've only just mentally adjusted to being back home and having a chance to be present for my family for the first time in … well, ever.

"The only other person I would have trusted with this is out of the country. You're the only choice. Once we get something signed off on, you can step back again. Maybe we can look at another monthlong stint in the—"

"I get it." I don't mean to snap, but *fuck*.

"Davey …"

"Don't. It's fine. I'll change my plans."

"As soon as it's done, we'll talk. I think it goes without saying that you've got a big bonus coming your way. You're irreplaceable. Your loyalty to the company is second to none."

That compliment, more than anything, makes me stupidly want to cry. And not in a good way. My loyalty to the company is great and all, but not when I don't give my family the same dedication. I hang up the phone, wishing I'd never answered. Maybe then I could have put off this conversation and kept playing perfect family.

Because that's all I'm doing. Playing.

I sink down into a crouch, phone *clunking* to the ground, and press my hands to my eyes. This is all part of the job. I know that. As marketing director, sometimes I have to do the shit that no one else wants to do—especially when it's the CMO asking. Six weeks at home is still better than the two or three I'm used to. It's practically a year in comparison.

Instead of focusing on the time I'll miss, I need to remember what I had. It's what I've done since I started this damn job.

I'll manage. It's a reflex to stamp the pain down at this point.

But I'm dreading telling Mack. I'm dreading leaving the kids. Maybe it was selfish of me to want so much time with them; they'll all just be getting used to having me here, and then suddenly, I'll be gone again.

But what other choice do I have?

Saying no will be seriously damaging to my career. If Eric is putting this on me, the account is clearly important, and fucking with something like that? Eric wouldn't even be able to save me if the higher-ups end up losing money.

My hands are tied, but I don't think Mack is going to get that. He never has. When it comes to my job, he doesn't want to hear how it works or have me defend the company. It's black and white in his eyes. It probably should be in mine as well.

I pick up my phone, picturing what would happen if I called Eric back and said no. If I emailed him my resignation right now. The hope that blooms in my gut is thwarted by all the what-ifs that plague me daily.

The same stupid thoughts I've been over more times than I can count.

Then I'm hit by a solid, undeniable thought that I've never let myself have before.

I can't do this anymore.

I can't.

Finally acknowledging that is like a dam of pressure flooding out of my system.

I thought I could have it all. I've clung, desperately, to this life I've built up for the four of us, but it doesn't matter how hard I push or how much I make, that life is getting away from me. These last few weeks have been too much. They've forced me to see what life should be like, and maybe finding something else will be more pressure. Maybe it will mean Mack has to get another job, or we'll need to sell the house or cut back on some things …

The thought of that financial pressure threatens to smother me, but before I let it take over, I shove it back again.

My thoughts stew, a lumpy mess of *mortgage, college, medical* that I can never seem to shut off.

Leaving my job means leaving those things in limbo.

I take a deep breath and stand.

Okay.

So.

I can't just quit. Spontaneity never suited me anyway.

But I *can* look for an out. Even if that means having to leave again right after Christmas, I'll be able to go knowing that this time it might be different.

I'll hang on to every moment with the three of them. Every giggle and every tear and every time Mack blushes. I'll use those memories to help me through the doubt. To push me through the moments when I remember how much I love my job and the people I work with.

They might be great, but my family is greater.

I need to remember that.

Starting right now.

I have three weeks to put feelers out for anything. I don't have to limit myself to Kilborough—Springfield might be an option. Hell, maybe even so far as New Haven. The commute would be a pain in the ass, but anything has to be better than what it is now.

Anything.

I take a deep breath and go join my family, no clue yet how I'm going to make this work.

But knowing that I have to.

16

Mack

Having the majority of our parties at Killer Brew really does make it feel like home. We've got the mezzanine above the bar, full drink service, with a towering Christmas tree standing in front of the mullioned windows.

I'm getting the warm fuzzies, which isn't just the alcohol talking.

But the alcohol is definitely talking.

I'm walking around, grin wide, feeling gooey and smiley and fuzzy—wait, I already said fuzzy. I throw back another swig of beer, loving the bubbly feel on my tongue.

Davey stuck close by earlier in the night, but he's chatting with Payne and Beau now, and I'm flitting from group to group, wishing I could sweep everyone up in a hug. I'm always happy, but tonight, that happy comes without a side of heartache, and I've gotta say, it's a nice change.

Having heart hurties is exhausting.

"Mack?"

I swing around and find Luke standing there. His cheeks and nose are flushed almost as red as his hair, so I assume he's only just arrived.

"Luke!" I throw my arms out and wrap him in a hug.

He laughs into my shoulder, hands resting on my back, and when I pull away, he's somehow even redder. "Ford and Orson said it would be okay to come."

"Yeah, of course. The more, the merrier! Get into the Christmas spirit." I almost knock into Keller—I definitely slosh the drinks he's carrying—as I scoop up a set of reindeer antlers. Then I turn back to Luke, step in close, and settle them on his head.

"Thanks." He touches the band gently. "Brayden didn't want to come tonight, so it's just me. Other than Orson and Ford, you're the only friend I have here. Any chance …"

"Yeah?"

"Well …" He gives a self-deprecating laugh. "Can you stick by me? For a bit while I meet people?"

"Of course. I'll introduce you around."

"Fuck, that'd be great. I've been here for most of this year and still haven't made a lot of friends. It's very different to back home, where I knew just about everyone."

"Why *did* you move here?"

Luke shrugs. "Job opportunity."

Something about that doesn't sound right. And normally I'm not the most switched-on bulb in the room, but I'm pretty fucking sure I'm reading this one right. "A job? What do you do?"

"Oh, uh …" He stuffs a hand in the pocket of his jacket and

rubs the back of his neck with the other. "I'm working as a tour guide. At Kill Pen."

"Oh, cool!"

He eyes me. "Really?"

"I bet it's the kind of job that's different every day. Is it spooky walking through all the cells, or have you gotten used to it by now?"

"I'm used to it." He studies me, smile pulling at his lips. "You're very animated tonight."

"Just a little tipsy."

His laugh is throaty. "I bet you don't get a chance to let your hair down much?"

"Nope! But it's fine. I love my kiddies and my husband, and work is great. Then I get tipsy when I can get tipsy."

Luke's giving me a strange look. "Husband?"

Shit. Did I say that out loud? "Ex! He's my ex. I said ex-husband."

"Of course you did." Luke's eyes flick to the other side of the room. "Well, don't look now, but I'm getting the feeling your ex doesn't like us talking."

"Really?" I swing around and find Davey in the same spot as before, hand wrapped around a glass, and glaring our way. As soon as our eyes meet, his dart away.

Luke pulls me back to face him. "I said don't look."

"But everyone knows when you say don't look, it obviously means you need to look."

"No, it literally means *to not to*." We're both snickering now. "Come on, I need a beer to be social."

"That sounds unhealthy."

"About as unhealthy as still being in love with your ex?" He gives me a pointed look.

"No. The beer thing is actually unhealthy. Physically. Mine's all mental, and it's totally fine because I know there's nothing there, and I'll move on when I want to move on. Easy peasy."

"Really?" His expression makes it clear he doesn't believe me as he calls over Lisa and orders for us both. "So it's a me thing, then?"

"What?"

"Well, I'd convinced myself that you never got back to me about a second date because you were still in love with your ex, but if you're not and it's *totally* easy to move on, then it must be me."

My mouth drops. "Not you. Of course not. I like you. You're funny and kind and weren't put off by all the, y'know, swelling." I still can't believe that our first date sent me into anaphylaxis. "You're great!" I drag the word out to emphasize that he is, in fact, great. Then I play punch his shoulder.

Luke looks from his shoulder to my face like he's about to laugh. "Stop that."

"What?"

"Trying to, I don't know, boost me up or whatever. If you're not interested, it's okay. I think you're cute, and I wanted to see where things would go, but I'm not all heartbroken or anything."

A long rush of air leaves me. "Well, that's a relief."

"I take it dating isn't something you do a lot of?"

"It's not something I do any of. Davey's home for two weeks, gone for two weeks. When he's home, we spend a lot of time together as a family. When he's gone, it's just me and the kids."

"You don't have family who can babysit?"

"Sure. Davey's parents." I don't even begin to explain how awkward it was that one time I asked them to watch Kiera and

Van so I could go out. Art had been determined to find me someone to sleep with—someone who wasn't their son—and my own pain was reflected in Mary's eyes. Handing off the kids was very much a silent conversation of "Oh, yes, here are the little ones. Please supervise while I get my dick sucked by someone who isn't your son," and then she'd silently said back, "We love you and want that for you but would much prefer it was our son doing the sucking," and I haven't been game enough to have that experience with them again.

Preferably ever.

"Are your parents not around?" he asks.

"They live in Boston, so we take the drive up there to see them, and they pop down from time to time, but for a sleepover? No go."

"I bet kids make everything so much harder."

"A lot." I palm my forehead, thinking of all the grays that have come through since that pair came into my life. "But also amazing too."

Luke turns this over for a moment. "I'm not sure I want kids."

"Any reason?"

"It's more a whole mesh of smaller reasons. And kids are something I don't think you should have unless you're one hundred percent decided on it."

"I agree." Davey and I had been on the same page every step of the way. The day we brought Kiera home, I don't think we took our eyes off her. She lived in our arms for the full two weeks that Davey was home, and then he left, and it was too hard for me to look after her and do everything else.

As bone-tired as I was, having her and Van is something I've never regretted, but it sure as fuck would be easy to.

"Your kids are super cute though," he says.

"Thanks. I know." They're adopted, but I like to take full credit for the cuteness that they are. "Let's say we dated." It's less of a segue and more of a steamroll. "You know the kids are a package deal, right? Like they won't be going anywhere."

His eyes crease at the corners as he takes another sip. "I'm not an idiot. And like I said, I'm not in love with you or have any grand expectations. All I wanted to know first is whether there could be anything there. If we'd worked out that it felt good between us, then we could have gotten into the deeper conversations. But let's say the guy I was into had kids, it's not a deal breaker. I'd adapt."

"Good to know."

Luke snickers a laugh into his drink. "Your ex *really* hates me, doesn't he?"

"What?" But before I can swing around this time, Luke grabs my arm and holds me steady.

"Do *not* look. Fuck me, Mack."

"Sorry."

"He's glaring though."

"How do you know? *You* didn't look."

"Just because I'm not as subtle as a bull doesn't mean I didn't look. I can see him in my periphery. He definitely wants to come over here and break things up."

"You think?"

"The jealousy is in neon."

I sigh, torn over whether that makes me happy or not. On the one hand, it shows he cares. I *know* he cares and loves me, but this is proof that he *loves me* loves me. On the other hand, I don't want him to feel jealous. It's a terrible, crummy emotion that I feel way too much of when it comes to him.

"Here's the thing: you're clearly still in love with him."

I don't answer, but it's not like I have to.

"It's okay. Well, from my side. From yours, it looks horrible, but I don't have to feel all that. The thing is, he sort of looks like he feels the same."

"I think he does."

"Then, sorry for being nosy, but why aren't you together?"

"His work." I down my beer, not liking that the fun, bubbly tipsiness has gone.

"That's right. He does something in PR?"

"Yep. He's always away, and it got too much for me, and he didn't want to choose us, so …" I trail off, remembering my conversation with Tonya about how drastically our lives would have changed if he made that choice. "It's not his fault. I don't think it's mine either. I think it's all a bit crap, and it wasn't supposed to work."

"Or …"

I cling to the word. "Yeah?"

"Well, as a guy, I know that if I lost someone and I still loved them, I'd be a bit of a territorial asshole. He didn't choose you, and even when you split, nothing really changed, right?"

"What's your point?"

"Change something, dammit!" Luke steps closer and drops his voice. "Go on a date with me."

"But—"

"At least that's what you'll tell him. We're friends, we can hang out—fuck knows I need some of those if I'm going to stick around here. I love Brayden, but it's getting like we're an old married couple."

"So … pretend to date, but not really?" I chew on that thought. "I don't like lying."

"Don't lie, then. Don't tell him we're dating. We'll hang out. Go to lunch, I'll pick you up for work on the days I start late, we'll catch up for breakfast or whatever. Then let Davey come to whatever conclusions he comes to."

As far as plans go, I hate it. But he's right that things need to change. I tried to romance him up, tried to make him fall back in love with the family life, and it hasn't worked. "Don't tell him we're dating, but let him think that we are?"

"Unless he asks you outright or whatever."

Not able to help it, I glance back over at where Davey is standing, and we catch eyes again. This time, he polishes off his drink and heads for the bathrooms behind the bar. I track every movement of his familiar gait, missing it more than ever.

"I want to actually go on a date," I say, feeling half-sick and half-relieved.

"You what now?"

"Like I said, you're a great guy. I'd be dumb to shut myself off to everything else on the slim hope that Davey will decide we're worth it. So let's try. Just the once. An actual date."

"An actual date."

"Will … will that be okay?"

Luke shrugs. "I know the deal, and you haven't lied to me about where your head is at, so let's go for it. If it doesn't work, we'll be back on my plan. Friends."

That bubbly, light, drunkish feeling creeps in again. I throw my arm around Luke's shoulders.

"Now that's out of the way, let's go make you some friends!"

17

Davey

MACK IS SLEEPING NOT GRACEFULLY. THE SNORING IS A DEEP rumble, he's got beer-morning breath, and where his arm is slung over my midsection is getting sweaty. I don't shift a single goddamn muscle.

By the time we got home last night, he was a stumbling mess, and I had to help him up to his room. The problem with that was being caught totally off guard by how much I miss when this room used to be ours, and he took that second of *ouch* to pass out onto me.

Platonic snuggles is something that I've been very careful not to let myself have, but with him curled into my side, clinging to me like a fucking Care Bear, I'm not moving in a hurry.

My hand finds his hair, stroking the short strands between my fingers as I ignore that serious tug in my chest.

I hardly got to see him last night. All his adorable drunkenness was given to Luke, and the two of them looked like they were having fun. It's been a long time since I've seen Mack laugh so much, and I was too much of a chicken shit to go anywhere near them.

The tension between me and my friends got so thick Art started spouting his "butterflies need to emerge" analogies that almost made me knock him over the head.

Mack stirs, rubbing his head into my hand like a puppy. Then, he lets out a loud groan that starts in his gut and goes on for way longer than it needs to.

"You good?" I ask as he turns his head and fake-sobs into my side. He's halfway down the bed, so it's easy enough to set my hand on his back and rub it for support.

"Sore. So sore."

"You did drink a lot."

"Why didn't you stop me?"

"Ah, let's think," I say. "Maybe because you're a grown man who knows how much he can handle and should be able to control himself."

"It's like you don't know me at all."

I chuckle but don't reply. We stay there in silence for a while, him not letting me go, and me indulging in the feel of his back muscles. I want to ask him about Luke and push to see what details I can get out, but firstly, he's hungover, and secondly, I really, really don't.

It's a twisted curiosity I know better than to think about but can't *stop* myself from thinking about.

"Want me to cook you something super greasy for breakfast?"

He moans, burying his face deeper. "Soon. Don't want to move yet. Too bright."

"You weren't *that* drunk."

"Think I was."

Maybe you shouldn't have let Luke keep buying them for you. I keep that thought to myself. On the off chance Mack was too drunk to remember, I don't want to be the one reminding him about his new boyfriend. "Guess you're getting too old to keep going out."

"Fuck you. You're older than I am."

"But I wasn't the one ten bottles deep and trying to sexy dance to Shakira."

"I fucking what?" His head pops up, skin a shade of green, deep circles under both eyes, and the usual clear blue gaze murkier than I've ever seen it.

I chuckle and uselessly brush his crushed hair back into place. "I haven't seen you move like that since our wedding day."

He lights up at the reminder, and we have a whole few seconds where everything feels right in the world.

Then he gets a text.

Mack jolts at the loud beep, and I scoop up his phone to pass over—knowing I shouldn't but not able to stop myself from checking the screen.

Luke.

He unwraps himself from me, and I throw my legs over the side of the bed.

"Right. I'll get breakfast started."

I stalk out of the room before he can read the message because I don't need to witness that. It's obvious, though, that Mack and I need to talk. About Luke, definitely. There needs to be some ground rules where he's concerned, but also about work.

And us.

Last night, I'd been ready to say fuck it and walk away from work for good, but I still need to find something else first, so there's no point in talking to him about my decision unless I'm sure it can go ahead. I know Mack, and I know that even if I tell him not to get his hopes up, his hopes will immediately fly anyway. His endless optimism is one of the things I love most about him.

I'd gotten complacent about *Luke* though.

I should have known better than to assume that because I hadn't seen him, and Mack hadn't been out anywhere, that his threat was gone. No, he's probably waiting in the wings until I leave again and he can swoop in.

Though he didn't have any issues *swooping* last night.

He's too young for Mack. He wouldn't know the first thing about what my husband needs. But apparently, he's going to try and come between us anyway, so this relaxed timeline I'd thought I had has been moved up.

Mack isn't waiting around for me to get my shit together anymore.

I don't blame him.

Well, *childishly*, I do. But I also know how misplaced that is.

And once I drop the bomb that I'll be leaving again a week after Christmas, I can't imagine Mack will be all that understanding.

Fuck, maybe I shouldn't tell him about that yet either. What if he gets upset and runs off crying to Luke and they kiss and … and …

I throw the frying pan on the stove, torturing myself with the image of the two of them together.

If I don't tell him about leaving now though, when the hell do I do it? Ruin Christmas and be all, "Surprise! My present is that I'm gone in a week!" Wait until after, when there are only a few days left? Wait until it's time to pack my bags?

The shower upstairs comes on, and I know that I have to do it now. Especially while Kiera and Van are out.

Looking back, one of the biggest issues in our marriage was that neither of us wanted to jump into the hard conversations. He'd hold it all in until it burst out of him, and I'd let him yell. Giving reasons always felt like excuses, and those excuses might as well have been given to the wall for all the good they did.

We got together young, and communication is something that didn't come easily to us.

Mack stumbles into the room, bundled up in an oversized hoodie and loose sweatpants. His hair is wet, and he's got more stubble growing through than usual, but fucking hell. My gaze rakes over him, hungrily remembering everything he keeps hidden under those clothes.

"That smells so good," he says, dropping down onto the stool closest to me. "I need all the bacon."

"I know." We might be terrible at communication, but I still know more about him than I ever want to know about another person. I move around the kitchen, frying up eggs, bacon, sausage, and mushrooms before getting us a stack of toast. Mack watches me the entire time.

I know bringing it up sooner than later is the smartest choice, but I don't want to break this quiet peace.

Also, with how hungover he is, it's probably better we get as much into his stomach as possible first.

I ignore that I'm nervous.

I ignore that I don't want to hurt him while ignoring that if he's *not* hurt, it'll kill *me*.

Emotions are horribly complex.

We settle at the table, and he dives straight in while I sip my very, very strong coffee.

I wait until he's downed at least a slice of toast and multiple rashers of bacon.

Then I say the worst words ever.

"We need to talk."

Mack looks up, mouth hanging open and half full of food. It should be a real turnoff.

It isn't.

"Uh-oh."

I manage a light laugh to ease the sudden tension. "It's nothing—" I was going to say "bad," but that would be a rotten lie. "Nothing serious. I have some not-so-great news, and we also need to talk boundaries."

"Boundaries?"

"Just … let's get the crappy news out first." My palms are clammy, and I'm nervous about how he's going to take this. Best case? Disappointed but supportive. Unfortunately, past experience does not give me hope.

Mack sets down his cutlery, and before I can say anything, he speaks. "You're leaving again, aren't you?"

My heart breaks at his tone. I was an idiot for thinking that he might not care because while he might be making an effort with Luke, the betrayal in his voice is real. Deep.

I take a long breath and try to get through this. "Not right away."

"When?"

"Second of January."

Devastation fills his face before he quickly masks it. "Right."

"Six weeks was still great though, wasn't it?"

One side of his lips makes a valiant effort to tilt upward. "Time with you always is."

"I'm sorry."

"I know. It's not your fault."

It sort of is though, not that I'll say that out loud. I'm itching to take his hand and tell him that while I might need to leave, I'm working on it, trying to find my way back to him. I hold it all in and force an upbeat voice. "Sorry it will cut into your time with Luke."

I think it's about the only thing I could have said to break through his disappointment. "What do you mean?"

"I know. That you two are …" I'm trying to be good about this, but it's fucking hard. "It's okay. You deserve everything, and I couldn't give that to you. Maybe he will."

"Hmm …" He gazes desolately at his plate.

"That's the boundary I wanted to talk to you about."

"What do you mean?"

"Him or … anyone. We've never talked about what happens when one of us starts dating. Now, I have nothing on the radar, I'm way too busy with work"—*and too in love with you*—"but it's clear you're ready. And I'll be supportive, I promise, but I … I can't see it, Mack." My voice breaks against my will. "Whether that means that you talk to whoever you're seeing and ask them not to come by the house, or I move out, or—"

"No."

"It was just a suggestion."

"You're not moving out. This is your home."

I sigh and look around because this house has my whole soul. "One day, it won't be. And we need to be prepared for when that happens."

He swallows thickly, blinking madly at his plate. "I won't date."

"Yes, you will. It's an awkward situation, but I understand. All I ask is you don't shove it under my nose, and, well, when it comes to the kids, I don't want people in and out of their lives. It's going to be confusing enough for them as it is, so please make sure that you're sure about whoever you introduce them to."

"That's fair."

I try to inhale, hoping that relief will take over, that the tension will finally leave. It doesn't. Even with that conversation out there, I feel worse than ever.

"Okay, well, that's all." I pile food I won't eat onto my plate, hoping it at least looks like things are back to normal.

Mack doesn't go back to eating. He nudges the food on his plate with his fork for a moment before his phone goes off again.

We both go stiff. I don't mean to, but without talking, it's clear we know who it is.

Mack doesn't make a move, so I know it's on me.

"You can get that," I whisper.

He leaves the table without a word.

18

Mack

My heart feels tender like a bruise as I kiss the kids goodbye and step aside, not wanting to meet Davey's eye. To his credit, he's been in a great mood all day, baking with the kids and building a fort in the living room.

This is a very, very bad idea.

I'd panicked when he said he only had two weeks left with us and texted Luke immediately to demand a date at his earliest convenience. Turns out that was only a few days away, and when I mentioned it to Davey, he didn't even blink.

No jealousy was had.

And that fucking sucks.

What the hell am I going out at all for if he doesn't care? I should be staying home with my family and soaking up all the time we can have together.

I can't shake the melancholy that's kicked in early this

time. We haven't told the kids he's leaving again yet, and I selfishly want to make him do it. The thing is, our reduced timeline has screwed me. In my plan to make Davey so jealous he stays, I'd thought it would be a gradual buildup instead of being dumped into the dating waters before I was ready.

And if he doesn't go for it, if he doesn't decide he suddenly needs to stay, then, well, I have to come to terms with packing up our lives to go with him.

The three weeks before he leaves again is nowhere near enough time to get me and the kids organized.

I gnash my teeth over the fact my life is Davey, Davey, Davey, and head for Luke's car. He's pulled up out the front of next door and waited in the driver's seat like I asked him to.

Because Luke is a really, really nice guy.

His smile is automatic when I climb in, eyes sweeping over me in an appreciative way I should like. But I don't.

Little by little, his smile ebbs.

"What's wrong?"

"Davey wasn't jealous."

There's a moment where he twists his mouth from side to side like he's not sure if he should answer or not. "The thing is, you're the one who said you wanted to try a date for real. Just one. So I think if we're going to do that, we need to not talk about Davey."

"But—"

"He's a huge part of your life. I get it. I also know the chances of anything happening here"—he swings a finger between us—"is slim. But if you want to actually try, just once, he needs to be out of the picture. We'll go on a date, we'll get to know each other, because I know there's a lot more about you than your ex-husband, then I'll drop you off and kiss you goodbye. Tomorrow, we'll chat. No matter how tonight ends, we're going to be friends."

The absurdity of the situation hits me all at once, and I start to laugh uncontrollably.

"You okay?" Luke asks, a shadow of his earlier smile popping up.

"Yep. I, uh, I don't know any other single person who'd agree to this. Why the fuck are you helping me?"

He shrugs. "Something to do."

"It's a big something."

Luke groans and drops his forehead against the steering wheel. "Well, you're hot, which definitely helps things, but— and I'm struggling with how to say this without it sounding weird—we're a lot alike." He stops abusing the steering wheel to look at me. "This sounds so stupid with all the drama surrounding your ex, but you don't seem like the kind of guy who likes that. I get the impression you're genuine, with a big heart, who just wants to be loved."

My neck heats under my collar. "Umm … yeah. Those were a lot of words."

"Sorry."

I appreciate everything he's doing for me, so the least I can do is make an effort too. With an almost panicky feeling, I slide the wedding band off my pointer finger and tuck it into my pocket. "I'm ready."

"Then can we go on our date, please?"

"You're the one driving."

He shakes his head, smile eating his face as he pulls out to drive to the restaurant, which, he assured me, does not specialize in foods that will send me to the ER tonight.

I get a flash of waking up to Davey waiting on me, and I

hurry to push it out again. Luke made a good point that if I want to give this a real go, Davey can't be on this date with us.

Luke deserves better than that, anyway.

Free Talk is a pretty little place with views of the water. Given it's Saturday, it's already busy, and we trail after the server who leads us to our table. We do the thing where the menus are dropped off and our water glasses are filled, and we nod and say thank you and avoid making eye contact.

Then we're left in silence.

And it occurs to me that the only conversational topics I have in mind involve the D-word.

And I don't mean dick.

"So … dick, huh?"

Luke almost snorts water from his nose. Through the coughing and hurrying to cover his face with a napkin, he gasps out, "*What*?"

"I'm sorry, I panicked."

"I figured." He finishes wiping his face and sets the napkin down. "Not what I was expecting you to say in a very full restaurant."

I palm my forehead. "I'm out of practice."

"And that was where you thought you should start?"

My cheeks are burning, but Luke's surprise gives way to amusement.

"So … about them." He pumps his eyebrows, and it helps me relax again.

"We are not off to a good start."

"Eh. I'm enjoying myself, and isn't that the whole point of dates?"

"I guess so."

Luke risks another sip of his water. "Now we've established where your mind is at, tell me some other cool stuff about you."

"I don't have anything cool, but …" I sift through my brain, trying to figure it out. The main things that jump out are Davey's work, the kids, Davey leaving, Davey dating, loving Davey. Fuck. When did that become my whole life? Talking about myself should be easy. The thing about being me is that I should know more about me than anyone, but I don't know anything at all.

Do … do I even exist?

I meet Luke's eyes. "I'm having the dawning realization that I don't actually have much of a life."

"What do you mean?"

"Tell me something about you. Really quick."

"I love cats."

"There. See?" I point at him. "That was so easy for you. I've sat here for, well, at least a minute, and I've got nothing."

"There's no way that's true."

"Apparently, I'm not a person anymore."

"Well, you're not a robot, so …"

"This is serious."

Luke reaches over to take my hand. He gives it a squeeze, and it feels nice. Surprisingly. "I imagine as a parent—a single parent most of the time—that you don't put much thought into yourself. But you're still you. That hasn't changed. I guess maybe you just need to remember who that person is."

I exhale deeply and tug my hand back. "Thanks. You're right."

"You like the Hobbit," he finally says.

"Yeah. Originally, it was *The Lord of the Rings* movies that got me into it all, but when I like something, I usually latch onto it. Went through so many behind-the-scenes videos, character interviews, then moved on to Tolkien biographies and loved all the stuff on the languages he created. I read the books, and then I read *The Hobbit*, and I dunno, I just loved it. It gave so much more context than the movies." I cut off when I realize I've said *a lot* of dumb words.

"That's so cool. Sometimes the background info on how something came to be makes it even more meaningful."

"Exactly."

"Is that why you work at the library?"

I take a drink, wondering how to structure my response without Davey coming into it. "Given I'm alone a lot of the time and my friends all work, once Kiera started school and Van was ready to be around kids his own age …" I lift a shoulder. "Needed something to do with my life. The job came up when I was searching, and it sounded perfect."

"Do you enjoy it?"

"I love it, actually." I think about the huge old building. The stacks of books. The wacky people we have in and the wild kids who either hang on to your every word when you read to them or tear the room apart. The more I think, the more I wonder if I really could walk away from all of that.

But … the alternative is losing Davey.

"Uh-uh," Luke jumps in. "I'm losing you."

"Sorry."

"Don't be. If I see you slip, I'll remind you again. I've got you."

"Thanks."

The waiter comes to take our orders, and the more we talk, the easier it gets, and the faster time gets away from us. Luke is right that he's a pretty open guy, and he knows exactly the right thing to ask or say in order to bring my personality out. Instead of leaving the date thinking I'm an empty shell of a man, my dusty brain is clicking over, and I'm remembering who I used to be.

Somewhere along the line, I lost that.

Now, I'm excited to find that person again.

With Davey, without him, that part is all still a mystery.

All I know is that I enjoyed myself with Luke, and while this isn't heading anywhere romantically, I like him enough that I need the night to think about it.

We pull up in front of my neighbor's house again, Luke creeping the car along so that we don't wake anyone up. It's almost midnight; we'd been talking so much, and I'm glad I got up the nerve to go.

"Whether you want to do that again or not," he says, putting the car in park, "I had fun."

"Me too."

"I hope you think some more. You're a cool person, and I know it sucks to feel lost and whatever, but you're not, really. Just … hiding." He grins, and I like that way of thinking about it.

"I'm glad we're friends."

His smile hitches, like he knows without me having to say much at all. "I'm pretty sure I said our date would end with a kiss good night."

The words settle between us. I'm weirdly nervous, and I'm not sure if it's because I want him to kiss me or I don't. The thing is, I didn't want to do any of this tonight, but I'm so glad I did. I'm walking away with a full brain and a lot of questions I wouldn't have if Luke didn't push me.

Do I want to kiss him? Not overly. But this is all part of it, isn't it?

Am I ready to move on?

Can I do it?

I like Luke as much as anybody, so kissing him will help me work out whether I'm wasting my time here. Can I really be open to someone who isn't Davey?

I fill my lungs and lean toward him.

Luke meets me halfway, our lips touching over the center console of his Ford something-or-other. I'm expecting more nerves. Butterflies, whatever. Instead, all I get is disappointment.

We both pull back at the same time, and he gives me a sad smile.

"We can't say we didn't try," he says. "I really, really hope you can work things out with Davey."

"Thank you."

Then I climb out of the car, for the first time in my life thinking clearer than I ever have. I *can* be open to someone who isn't Davey. I just don't want to.

I'm done expecting Davey to solve our problems for us.

It's my turn to fix things.

19

Davey

I'm sitting at the dining room table when Mack walks in, the clothes dryer a low hum in the background. It's late and he's quiet, but the light must clue him in to my still being awake because his head pokes around the door a minute later.

"Davey?" His tone goes up. Less of a question and more … do I hear guilt? Or do I only want to hear guilt?

Fuck, I shouldn't have looked. Shouldn't have poked my head out the window, waiting for him. Then I never would have seen what I did.

"What are you doing up?" Mack asks, stepping into the room, big coat swamping him, nose bright red.

"Couldn't sleep."

"Oh."

"I'm fine."

His silence hangs between us. A huge question mark

asking so many things we both know I can't answer. Their date must have been good to end with a kiss good night, and I know I need to say something because the elephant in the room keeps getting bigger.

All I have to do is check he had a nice time. Tell him the kids went down easily. Make sure Luke treated him right. Instead, I notice his wedding band missing from his finger, and what comes out of my mouth is "He looked like a good kisser."

And I can't say I loved the tone I used either.

Mack's face falls. "You saw that."

"Heard a car and wanted to make sure it wasn't someone turning up to rob the neighbor. It's late, after all."

His usually sweet, happy face turns stormy. "You said you didn't care if I went out."

"I don't." I push up from the table so that we're both standing.

"Kinda sounds like you care."

"I guess I didn't realize how late dates go these days, that's all."

He snorts, and it's heavy with derision.

"What's that supposed to mean?" I ask.

"It's supposed to mean *bullshit*. Which is all that's coming out of your mouth."

"Bit hard for me to know what happens on a date when I can't remember the last one I went on."

Mack scoffs and moves into the kitchen, heading for the cupboard he keeps the glasses in. "Maybe you should check your MyMatch profile. I'm sure it will have the whole history on there."

My … Air rushes into my lungs. How the fuck did he find

out about that? Mack isn't on the app. I checked. He's always been very anti-meeting people online.

He fills his glass and takes a long gulp, then sets the cup down heavily. "Yeah. I know. You've dated. So don't be a hypocrite."

"A hypocrite? I talked to a handful of men on there when I thought it would help me get over you! Do you have any idea the type of hole you left in me when you asked for a divorce? Signing those papers was the single hardest thing I've ever done in my life, Mack. Fuck."

"R-really?"

"You know it was. Come the fuck on."

"I … I thought you'd be happy. At least if you're not tied down to me, you can hook up with men in whatever cities you were in and not be held back by the old guy in a small town."

Old guy? Held back? Fury rings in my ears. "What the *fuck* are you talking about?"

He averts his gaze. "I know you didn't feel the same way about me as when we first got together. You never wanted sex when you were home, and it was like … like I was … in your way."

"I was fucking tired! Between travel, work, and young kids, I was maxed out."

He squares his jaw determinedly. "It was more than that."

"Now who's talking complete bullshit?"

He whirls on me and crosses the kitchen to get in my face. "You think the divorce was easy for me? All I wanted was for you to choose us. I never actually thought you'd agree!"

I stare at him. One beat … two. I'm so stunned I forget to be angry. "Tell me you didn't suggest getting a divorce *on a whim*?"

Mack's face falls. "Ah … well, maybe."

"You didn't want to get divorced?"

He swallows. "I guess I didn't know how deeply ruined our relationship was. I didn't know you were that ready to go through with it."

Two years. I've lost two whole years, countless memories, and piled up way too much angst, all because I called a bluff neither of us knew he was making. I love Mack, but dear fucking god, do I want to strangle him right now. "You said you couldn't do this anymore!"

"I would do anything for you." His eyes are reddening, like he's holding back tears. "All you had to do was say no. All you had to do was show me that I'm the person you fell in love with. Instead, you agreed so fucking fast it's like you'd been waiting to bring it up yourself."

"I just wanted to make you happy instead of miserable all the damn time."

"Well, congratulations. Because I've been miserable ever since you left." He spins on his heel and leaves the room. A moment later, I hear him jogging up the stairs.

My heart is getting away from me, beating so fast in anger and regret and all the unspoken what-ifs that Mack left behind. While I'm drowning in the urge to pick up his empty glass and smash it, the indignation is struggling to hold on. Because he was right. Our marriage was at a breaking point, even if neither of us realized it. It's hard not to feel like we divorced for absolutely no reason, but if the last two years have given me anything, it's clarity.

We wouldn't have been able to sustain what we had.

We can't go back to that either.

Feeling like I'm on the edge of useless tears, I bypass the laundry to grab his pajamas I was warming up and climb the stairs. His bedroom door is closed, and I can't make out any noise coming from inside.

Trying to smother down my simmering frustration that we can't get our heads out of our asses, I tap lightly on the wood.

"What?"

Bracing myself, I push it open.

He's sitting on the side of the bed, clearly having run his hands through his hair a billion times. Without words, I step forward and hold out his warmed clothes.

Mack's mouth hangs open as he takes them. "I miss that, you know. When you're not here."

I shrug awkwardly. "You're always cold."

"Feeling colder than ever right now." He sets the pajamas down beside him, then holds out his hand.

I take it eagerly, gut swooping at his warmth. At the familiarity.

He doesn't stop pulling me closer until I'm standing between his legs. Then he sets his hands on my hips.

"What are you doing?"

Mack's thumb slips under the bottom of my shirt and finds the soft skin above my hip. "You never used your profile?"

"Never."

"Never dated?"

"Not even once."

"That doesn't mean you—have you ever, you know, seen anyone else?"

I feel like an idiot for admitting this, but I hold his eye and shake my head. "There's been no one but you."

"Oh, thank god." His forehead drops to rest on my diaphragm. "I couldn't look at another man. Then Art said you probably had, and I got in my head about it—"

"I'm gonna kill Art."

"Can I help?"

My hands find his face, and I tilt it up to look at me. Mack doesn't hold back how he feels. His eyes are open and honest, mixed with awe and love and everything that's always made me feel like a better person than I am.

His face is scruffy like always, neat stubble that scratches my palms, and I ache to feel it in other places. Every place.

I duck my head until our lips touch, and it's torture. I'm about to pull back again when Mack grips the front of my shirt, holding me in place.

"Again."

"Mack …"

"Kiss me." He sounds so desperate there's no way I can say no.

My lips crush his, hard and needy, and Mack gives me the same passion right back. There's something about the way he kisses that ticks every box for me, and no matter how many times I kiss him, the result is the same.

Pure ecstasy.

His strong tongue skims mine, and I groan as he deepens things, one hand wrapped around the back of his neck to anchor him, to keep him here with me.

From what I could see, his kiss with Luke was nothing like this.

And how could it be? No one can give Mack what he needs the way I can, and if I wasn't so fucking in love with this man, I'd shake him for putting us in this position.

Where we're in love and divorced.

So, so in love.

My feelings for him have never dulled; it was them that pushed me to do better, to be better. All I've ever wanted out of life was to give this man everything he needs.

Mack breaks the kiss, fingers knotted in my hair, lips trailing over the freckles on my nose like he always used to do, and says, "I want your lips around my dick."

My cock swells at those words. "Want to blow in my mouth, baby?"

"Please." Mack reaches for his belt, clumsily tugging it undone. "I've missed it so much."

Seeing the way he needs me has my heart pounding erratically. I strip off my shirt and go for my pants, watching as Mack reaches into his and pulls his dick out through his fly. If he thinks I'm not getting him completely naked, he's wrong.

I shove my underwear down and off and straighten to Mack licking his lips, eyes locked on my erection.

"Missed him too?" I ask.

He squirms to the edge of the bed, and I give myself a lazy tug as I step closer. Then, before he can lean forward and take me in his mouth, I drop to my knees.

"Take your shirt off."

"Davey …" He reaches for my dick, but I grab his hand and pin it to the bed.

"Now."

The frustration is clear as he unbuttons his shirt and then tosses it aside. "Better?"

"Not yet." I grab his pants, and he lifts his ass as I slide them off. As soon as I have Mack on full display for me, I sigh. He's perfect.

And so is his cock.

Not wanting to wait anymore, I lean forward and suck him into my mouth. His taste, the way he stretches my lips wide, how his fingers twist into my hair. I sink down lower, tongue sliding along his shaft until his head bumps the back of my throat.

"Fuck, Davey. You look so good on your knees for me."

This is where I was meant to be. Where our relationship was always supposed to be fulfilled to capacity. All the casual touches, and teasing, and affection, and frustrations … it all reaches completion the moment we're naked and alone, indulging in everything the other has to give.

I don't go all out to start with. Just tease him and taste his skin. Collect every drip of precum that hits my tongue. I pay his balls as much attention as his cock, using my hands and mouth to make him feel good. There are light scratch marks down his thighs, and it's so hard to stay on task when his ass is *right there.* All I'd have to do is throw his legs over my shoulders and go to town on his ass.

But his dick is tonight's focus.

I release his ball I'm sucking on and lick a stripe along the underside of his shaft instead. So pretty, he has my dick aching, and before I go back to sucking him off properly, I spit in my hand and wrap it around my cock.

The relief is instant.

With a moan, I get started on him again. Mack is rocking his hips, heavy breathing music to my ears. The way he murmurs my name lights a fire in my rib cage, and I'd do anything to bottle this moment. To always have the reminder of how good we are together.

I suck him down until his cock fills my throat, jerking fast at how wholly he fills me. It's a delicious stretch, quickly stealing my oxygen, but then I hear a *"oh, shit, Davey,"* and I know I'd rather pass out than pull off right now.

I love this man so much it hurts.

"So close," he gasps. "Fuck. Nearly there."

I pull back a little, just in time for his cum to flood my mouth. I swallow down every drop he gives me, loving the way his dick pulses in my mouth a couple of times before going still. Once he's done, I stand.

With one hand strangling my cock, I tilt Mack's face up to me with the other. His eyes are wonderfully unfocused, and I capture his mouth in a kiss. I keep him there, mouths fused together, slipping closer and closer to the edge myself.

Mack's breathing heavily into the kiss, and I know he can taste himself on me. It's something that used to drive him wild, and it makes me hornier than ever to tease him with it now.

My dick is almost painfully full, ready to shoot. The need is building at the base of my spine, and when Mack reaches up to cup my balls, it's all over.

I growl into our kiss as I mark him. Each rope of cum is lovingly milked onto his skin, deliberately making sure that every last drop hits him. He's mine. Skin, muscle, bone. Every piece that makes him up belongs to me, I can feel it. Right in my core. I rub the head of my cock into the mess until I'm too sensitive for more.

Then I straighten, panting as much as he was before. My head is spinning that we went there again, but this time, I don't doubt for a second whether that should have happened.

This time, there are no doubts.

It wasn't a mistake.

Mack holds my eyes as he slowly rubs my cum into his skin. "I'm not showering tonight," he says.

And he doesn't.

20

Mack

The whole morning at work, I can't stop smiling. Davey and I want to be together, so I'm going to make it work. After setting up for the knitting club, I return to my desk and open my old pal Google.

The determination is thrumming in my veins, and I think I'm scaring Tonya by how upbeat I'm being. I'm never normally in a bad mood, exactly, but ever since Davey got home, I've been … unsettled. With all these what-ifs in my brain, it feels like my head is too full, and I'm so focused on the stuff floating through it to worry about things like smiling at people and not constantly whining.

But today, I'm so happy I can feel it in my bones.

I spoke with Luke earlier, and we agreed that while the date was fun, there was nothing romantic about it. I'm still glad it happened, though, because it was a real slap to the face to remember I used to be a whole person, and I'm getting the sneaky feeling that I put so much pressure on Davey being here for me because I wasn't here for myself. He was my life raft.

That's not how a relationship is supposed to be.

I keep going to twist my wedding band around my finger, but I haven't put it back on yet, and I'm not sure I want to. If I'm going to be me, I need to let go of our failed marriage and focus on what comes next.

Me:

What's ONE hobby you guys like to do?
Payne:
Art, don't say s—
Art:
Sex.
Payne:
You were asking for that one.

I laugh because he's right. When it comes to Art, I know I need to be more specific.

Me:

Fine. Because someone needs guidelines, something other than sex or anything sexual or immature or gross. Things that would be listed specifically as hobbies in the dictionary.
Griff:
I don't think you know how dictionaries work.
Orson:

What's going on? This is a random question even for you.

Me:

I went out with Luke and when he asked me to talk about myself, I had nothing. I don't want to have nothing.

Payne:

As in things that we do in our free time, just for us? Beau colors in. I like to go for a run or play with my nieces. Plan out more fun for Killer Adventures.

Me:

See? See how easy that was for you?

Orson:

Are we going to skip over the part where you went out with someone who wasn't Davey?

Me:

That's not important.

Keller:

Considering Davey's all we've heard about for the last few weeks and you're still madly in love with him, it's kind of important.

I TAKE A MEASURED BREATH, TRYING NOT TO GET FRUSTRATED. I've already mentally moved on from all of this, but I suppose reading my mind isn't something they've mastered yet, which seems like an oversight on their behalf.

ME:

I wanted to see if it was possible to move on. It isn't. Luke and I are happy as friends. Davey never wanted to get divorced, and then we had sex, and I've decided I'll be traveling with him when he leaves, but I want to work out all the details first before I say anything. Before all that, I need to make sure I have a life outside of him. Apparently that's something I've lost, and I'd like to not be a terrible partner when I'm following him all over the country. All caught up?

Payne:

I have so many questions.

Me:

Well, put a pin in it. Hobbies, please?

Orson:

I like to dance. Ford has his cars he works on.

Griff:

I whittle.

Keller:

Work out, do crosswords, cook.

Me:

See? I don't have any of that! Davey has his LEGO, and I cook because I like being the one to feed my family, but I hate the actual cooking part

Orson:

You like to read though, right?

THE QUESTION CATCHES ME OFF GUARD. I'M NOT SURE WHEN I would have even mentioned that to him, or maybe Orson just picks up on things most people don't.

ME:

I used to. It's been a while.

· · ·

My gaze runs over the rows and rows of books all around me.

Me:

With the kids, I'm always getting interrupted. So I sort of gave up trying. The thought of getting into it again is ... intimidating.

Art:

Because you're placing too much pressure on it. You're not getting into it "all," you're picking up a book. One book. Then maybe opening the cover. This isn't a fucking marriage, it's a hobby, and for what it's worth, I agree. You do need your own thing. Joey and I have separate lives outside of each other, and it means we always have stuff to talk about. Being apart makes us stronger together.

I'm stunned as I read over the message. Art's managed to put into words exactly what I've been struggling with. I don't want the same physical distance as before, but Davey always got to be his own person, and I think I resented that. I never asked him about his job, and when he tried to talk to me about things, I didn't want to hear it.

Fuck, even when he said he had to go back early, I completely shut down.

While I was stewing at home because I was overworked, what the hell was Davey going through?

That's it. No more. I'm fixing my shit and no longer blaming Davey for our relationship problems.

. . .

PAYNE:

I don't know whether to be impressed by Art's message, or make a call for a welfare check.

Art:

Penisssss.

Orson:

There he is.

I SMILE AND POCKET MY PHONE. THAT MIGHT HAVE BEEN A tangent I wasn't expecting when I messaged them, but Art confirmed my thoughts, and Orson nudged me in the direction I was avoiding thinking about myself.

I leave my desk and the *how to homeschool* tab behind and make my way into the stacks. We've got our history and geography sections up front and most of the fiction down the back. Tonya's always sneaking in time to read at work for *research*, so there's no reason why I can't do the same whenever I get a free five minutes.

The fantasy aisle calls to me, and I step into it, breathing in the smell of books. Chatter from the knitting club just behind me breaks up the silence. I run my fingers along spine-cracked books, hoping that one will jump out at me. Anything.

I could pick up *The Hobbit* again, but the thought of diving into something that detailed makes me exhausted already. Am I in the mood for dragons? Epic fantasy? Intricate worldbuilding? I'm waiting for an impulse, for my hand to find a book and be like "this one," but that doesn't happen.

There are too many, and I'm overwhelmed by the choices available. Maybe I should have googled this too? For a librarian, I really don't have up-to-date knowledge on the new bookish trends.

Fuck, am I a bad librarian as well as a bad husband? All I need is to be a sucky dad as well for my whole life to crumble apart.

Already overwhelmed, I drop down to the floor and lean against the books behind me, craning my neck to look up at all the options.

"Oh, there you are, love. We're off," Judith says, pausing at the top of the aisle. She's got a pink rinse in her hair, and her knitting glasses are still on, making her look slightly bug-eyed. "Come now, why are you on the floor?"

I smile up at her. "Just thinking."

"And it's easier from down there, is it?"

"It's more that the weight of it all got me into this position."

Judith tsks. "My husband used to say you've gotta keep a strong back. You're not going to get one all hunched over like that."

Ignoring the generational gaps in that comment, I change the subject. "I thought you still had another half an hour."

"Well, we were supposed to, but then Freida got on Maree about whose quilt was going to be voted first at the fair, and it became a whole thing. The two of them are like bulls locked at the horns. I'll never understand it, myself." She turns her nose up. "Always been perfectly agreeable. My husband always used to say, delicate like a flower, I am."

If there's anything Judith isn't, it's a flower. "Thanks for letting me know. I'll go and deal with the room."

"Good lad. We'll see you next week."

She bustles away, and I sigh, pushing myself up from the floor, about to grab a random book and take a gamble.

Then, an author's name catches my attention.

Beau Rickshaw.

Holy fuck. Beau! I'd always planned on picking up something of his, but then life filled up, and it totally slipped my mind. I have no idea what these books are about, but a quick glance at the blurb looks promising. Not quite Tolkien heavy, but definitely some sort of fantasy aspect.

I tuck it under my arm, then deal with the pitchers of water and empty glasses in the meeting room before setting it all back out into its generic layout. We don't have to use it again until a meeting tomorrow, so I lock up and walk back out to my desk, flipping through the book. It's got a bio of Beau inside the back cover, and it's so weird to see someone I know smiling from the inside of a book.

This is freaking cool.

Am I nervous I won't like it? A little bit. But if I don't mention to him or Payne that I have it, we don't need to deal with that awkward conversation if the book isn't for me. I'm well aware I'm putting a lot of pressure on my friend to get me back into something I used to love, so he doesn't need to know that too.

I drop down into my desk chair and wake up my computer before I turn to set the book down again. Except there, in the spot I was going to set it, is a copy of *The Hobbit*.

I frown at the offending book, not finding it so cute this time. Luke and I *agreed* to be friends. That's it. So if there's another cutesy love note in there, that's going to confuse the hell out of me. I'll probably have to have an awkward conversation, and then how do I even be friends with him if I don't trust him to drop it?

Right before I can cross into actual stress mode, I pick up the book to see if there's even a note in this one.

And of course there is.

Fuck. Right. Well.

I can either ignore it, or I can check and hope that it's a platonic message full of totally bro type of, umm, things. A Merry and Pippin of notes, if you will.

I brace myself and pull out the scrap of paper, gaze scanning over the words and gut slowly collapsing out through my ass.

Bilbo didn't give up. And neither will I.

Well, fuck.

That doesn't sound good.

Either this is from Luke and I really, really misjudged the man.

Or it's from someone else and I'm going to end up in their basement somewhere.

I pull out my desk drawer and stow that note on top of the others, reasoning that this could be a very old note, and maybe I've been too distracted to notice the book sitting there before today. If Luke left it before our date, that's totally not a single problem. Probably.

Focusing on work doesn't come easily for the rest of the day.

21

Davey

"GOOD MORNING," I CALL OUT TO ART AS I CROSS KILLER Brew. I've already dropped the kids off, and Mack is at work, so I'm free to commit third-degree murder if it comes to it. "I'm giving you a choice. Either I kill you for getting in my husband's head about me sleeping with other men, or you help me. You have until three to answer. One … Two …"

"Hold up," Joey says. "Why are you killing Art? What did he do?"

"He told Davey he should find someone to hook up with because that's what I would be doing."

Joey turns his glare on Art. "I wish this surprised me."

"Well, how was I supposed to know?"

"You could have asked," I point out.

"Sure. I'm going to say, 'Hey, Davey, who've you fucked lately?'"

"You say that like it isn't a standard opening for you."

At least he has the good sense to look sheepish.

Joey looks torn. "Are you upset that he slept with someone? Because even though Art's a dumbass, I don't think you can blame him for that."

"No. Thankfully, Mack didn't sleep with anyone. And neither did I. But he was hurt because he thought I did."

Joey pulls the dish towel from his shoulder and whips Art across the ass with it.

"Fucking *ouch*!" he cries. "But also … do it again."

"*Don't* do it again. Die or help? Two and a half … thhhhh—"

"Fine. I'll help." Art's handsome face morphs into something that might look like disappointment if his eyes weren't so amused. "You don't need to threaten me. I'll do it anyway."

"This way was more fun for me." I settle on the stool, and Joey pours me a Coke.

"You're paying for that," Art says as I take a sip.

Joey winks. "I've got it. Art loves when I buy other men drinks."

He huffs but comes over to sit next to me. "What do you need help with?"

"I'm moving home."

"Uh … what?"

My fingers drum over the hard bar top, and the words are difficult to get out, but I'm determined. "I love my job, but they're pulling me back into the office over a month earlier than we agreed on, and if I'm honest … I'm tired. I'm tired of leaving the kids. I'm so, so tired of leaving Mack. The travel is amazing, and I get a lot out of what I do, but there comes a point where I have to admit that I can't have it all."

Art looks like he doesn't know what to say. There's no sign of joking when he says, "But you love your job."

"Yeah. I do."

"You love your family more."

"Obviously."

Joey crosses his arms and leans toward us. "What's changed though? No offense, but I'm pretty sure you've always loved your family more. It'd be shitty of you if you didn't."

I huff a laugh, not offended, because he's right. "I took them for granted. Even after the divorce, Mack was always there. We were still together whenever I was home. Still happy, still playing the part of a family for the kids."

"And?"

I screw up my face. "He went on a date the other night, and it was the first time I've had to face what life would look like if he moved on."

"Ahh … the old 'don't know what you have until it's gone' trick."

That's so far from wrong I don't know where to start. "I've always known what I have. Mack is the most kindhearted, incredible man. I love him. I've never stopped. But the thing is … I don't have him anymore. Not really. And the reality of that cuts me up inside."

"So you're moving home." Art thinks it over for a moment. "I don't think that's a good call."

"What?"

He looks world-weary as he shrugs. "That's not to say I don't think the two of you together is for the best. It is. You were made for each other. But if you're anything like me …" He waves a hand over the bar. "I am this place. I am my work. I love that about me, and Joey would never try to change it. If he did, well, I don't think we'd have the shot at forever that we do because I wouldn't be me. And he wouldn't be him."

"I don't want to be my work."

"You are though. What you want doesn't matter."

I'd been so confident with my plan when I walked in here, and I hate that Art is hitting me with the truth. "What am I supposed to do? Let him go? Give up on my family?"

He opens his mouth and quickly shuts it again.

Dammit, no. I'd had a plan, and I'm sticking with it. I've been back and forth over this enough. "I know what you're saying, but I'm done. No more. I'm not walking out on work tomorrow, but I *am* going."

"Right. So what do you need me for?"

"Your contacts."

"Ah. I have those, do I?"

"You wouldn't be the great Art de Almeida, future ruler of the universe, if you didn't."

He nods. "Flattery will get you everywhere. I'll make some calls."

And while he does that, I'll mindlessly troll every job listing that's driving distance away. Even ridiculously long commutes are an improvement to what we're going through now.

On the way home, I pick up a box of Mack's favorite donuts and then straighten up the house a bit. With the free time I have left, I head out to my LEGO shed. Everything is exactly where I left it. Honestly, I haven't spent as much time out here as I used to. And *honestly*, honestly, a lot of the time I spent in here was to get some distance from Mack.

The tension was thick before the divorce, and I didn't want to deal with it, so this was the way I switched off. Standing here now, the itch to build something isn't what it used to be. I still love it, still regret my Millennium Falcon being smashed, but this particular room … it makes me sad.

I switch off the light and step back outside. There's a room in the house where I could relocate all my things, but that comes with the added risk of the kidlets breaking something again. And even if I did move inside, what would I do with the shed?

The weight building over my shoulders suddenly releases with the reminder that I have *time*. I don't have to figure it all out now. Soon, I won't be packing my suitcase and leaving every couple of weeks. Goodbye frequent-flier miles, goodbye hotel rooms, goodbye that deep ache in my chest every time I have to leave my family again.

It's fucking cold because it snowed last night, and I'm getting hopeful it might stick. Some of the best memories of my childhood were going to sleep on Christmas Eve, belly full of Gran's casserole and pudding, then waking to presents and snow covering everything. Somehow, it made Christmas more magical. I want that for Kiera and Van. I sort of want that for me too.

But Gran's gone, and Kilborough hasn't had a white Christmas for at least five years, so I'm not hopeful this year will be the one. With a fifty-fifty shot, it's got to be coming soon though, and hell—I tilt my head back to look at the bleary gray sky—maybe it could be my sign. A way of showing me that this is where I'm supposed to be. I'm making the right choice.

By the time I'm back inside, my hands are frozen solid, so I make a coffee, grab my laptop, and then sit down to job hunt. It's been so long since I've had to do this that I'm rusty as fuck. I also don't have an updated resume since my job has never been in danger of going somewhere, and I've never wanted to let that kind of job security go.

The problem is, this close to Christmas, businesses are wrapping up for the year. There are no jobs in my field advertised and barely any outside of last-minute retail at all.

Okay.

This isn't going to be a quick thing.

I knew that.

My first steps are to make up a resume, maybe look up some of the people I've met at conferences over the years to see if they're, A, close, and B, willing to make some introductions between me and their HR departments. Then, I should tackle our budget. If I'm going to take a pay cut, I need to know how much of a reduction we can manage without making major changes to our lives.

It's looking more and more that returning to work on the second will be unavoidable, but at least this time I can go, knowing we'll have a better future ahead.

22

Mack

My eyes get wider and wider the further I read. I haven't been able to put Beau's book down. Not only has the plot got its hooks into me, but … damn. I didn't know he was so filthy.

My cheeks are burning up, and it's not because of the fire.

I take it back. There's nothing Tolkien about this book.

"You okay?" Davey asks.

I glance up, forgetting to close my mouth, and stare at him. "Uh …"

Suspicion crosses his face. "What are you reading over there?"

"Ah, nothing! It's totally, umm, like … dragons. There's a dragon. And these, umm, magical monkeys …"

He gets up, smile slowly creeping across his face, and drops down into the spot beside me. His dark freckles are extra obvious up close, and I remember running my lips over them the other night. I want to do it again. "Let me see."

"See …"

"Your book. I want to read it."

"Ah. No. You don't read."

"Not usually, but I'm curious now."

"I told you it was nothing." I clutch the book to my chest, mortified over the idea that he'll catch me reading something so … so … smutty. Trying to tell him that everything up until this point has been amazing worldbuilding will be useless when he sees a page full of cock.

"Right."

I go to stand, but Davey yanks me back down again and wrestles the book out of my grip. He finds the page I had open and—one hand holding me back, and the other stretched out away from me—he starts to read. "… *splitting him wide with his cock and pushing until he was seated in divine comfort. The pair cradled each other close as Jaciel's whimpering exhale breezed over his lips …*"

Davey turns slowly, eyes wide, face reflecting all the exact same shock that played over mine minutes before. "Porn. You're reading porn."

"Fuck off." I snatch the book back. "This is the first sex scene, and it caught me by surprise too."

Davey's shock wears off. "That's kinda hot."

"What?"

"Are all books like that?"

"No. At least, none of the ones I've ever read before."

"Well, damn. I probably could have gotten into *The Hobbit* more if it'd had the dwarves all banging each other."

My gaze snaps to him. "What did you say?"

His lips twitch. "Just pointing out that if the king was

banging more people, he probably wouldn't have been so uptight."

"Right …"

"I'll have to message Payne and find out if he knows his boyfriend is such a deviant."

I huff and toss the book aside. "I was enjoying that, and now you've ruined it."

Davey leans forward to pick it up, then sets it back on my lap. "I'm only teasing. I think it's cool you're reading Beau's book." He runs his fingers along the spine. "Actually, I don't think I've seen you read in a while."

"I haven't," I confess. "I'm trying to get back into it. This is the first book I've read in … too long."

"In that case, I'm doubly sorry for the teasing," he says seriously. "You used to read all the time when we met. I still remember having to use sex to distract you from the damn books."

"Hmm … those were the days."

They really were. Things weren't exactly *not* complicated, but we were happy. Too young and dumb to know where we were heading. If we'd known we were going to get divorced, would we have still gotten married?

I slide my hand over Davey's stubble, and his eyes fall closed as he leans into the touch.

It gives me my answer instantly.

Yeah, I still would have married him, because that's what got us to this exact moment.

My thumb lightly strokes the spiky hairs, and it brings a small smile to his lips.

"Tell me about work," I whisper.

Davey's eyes fly open, and I hate that there's worry there. "What?"

"What's your favorite thing about it?"

"Ah …" He clears his throat and pulls back, breaking contact between us. "It's … good."

The fact he can't even talk about it makes me feel guilty. It makes me hurt for that dark place we got to. But I know better now, and I'm going to do better. Starting with this. "Really. I want to know what you love about it. Like, for me … I love that even though I wasn't reading, working at the library kept me connected to books in a way. I love chatting with the people who come in, and it's always fun to come up with new ideas to get the community involved." I try to show him with my eyes that I'm serious. No hidden motive. No agenda. I just want access to that side of him again.

"Well, I have a team now …"

I nod, encouraging him to keep going.

"It's pretty cool to manage a whole department. Obviously, a lot more stress, but …"

"What's stressful about it?"

His eyes search mine, and I understand why he's cagey. Do I want to hear about everything so great and wonderful that keeps pulling him away? Absolutely not. But I also need to stop making everything about me.

"For one thing, if someone else fucks up, it's on me. If we lose a big contract, or the client is unhappy, or we blow out the budget—all me. It means I need to be communicating hard with everyone, but there's also a layer of trust involved to stop me from micromanaging. Taking that step back was difficult."

"Sounds tough."

"Yeah …"

"Probably even more tough without a supportive family behind you."

"What? No." Davey wraps my hand in his. "You've always been more supportive than I deserved."

I squeeze his hand back, knowing that I don't ever want him to feel that way again. "No. We both fucked up in different ways, but I'm sure we can agree that I'm the one who pulled away. You might have physically left, but you always came back. I put that wall between us."

Like he can't stop himself, Davey shifts forward, face burying into my shoulder. I wrap my arms around him and hold him close. This is how we're supposed to be.

"I didn't want to hurt you anymore," he whispers.

"You know what I really, really want?"

He glances up again, face so close I could kiss him. Those warm brown eyes search mine. "What?"

"To let it go."

His eyebrows flex in question.

"I think it's time we put it all behind us. I want to move on. I want to do that with you, however that looks for us. Friends, boyfriends, husbands. I don't care. I'm working on myself, for you, for the kids, for me. I want to be happy again. But I can't keep relying on you to be the one to do it."

"But I want to make you happy."

"I know, and you do. But you can't be the *only* one. It's too much pressure."

"So … we just … move on."

I cup his face again. "You okay with that?"

"Yes, but … nothing's actually changed. I'm still leaving in a few weeks."

"Yeah, and it's going to hurt. But I don't want you to think that you can't talk to me if you need to. Like you said, your job is stressful, and you have a lot of responsibility on your plate. Let me help you."

Davey's shaking exhale is the only sound between us for so long.

"I'm going to come with you," I whisper.

"What?"

"I looked up homeschooling today. And how it would work if we could do half and half, but—"

His mouth crashes down on mine, hands finding the back of my head as he holds me to him. Davey makes no move to deepen the kiss, just keeps us pressed together in the type of connection we've missed for so long. I revel in it, heart soaring, hoping that this is it. This is the moment where everything makes sense again. "You're the most amazing person I've ever known," he murmurs.

I hurry to shake my head. "It's the right thing to do."

Davey pulls back, slowly, like he doesn't want any distance between us. "I'm sorry, but it isn't."

"What do you mean?"

"We can't do that to Kiera and Van. And you can't leave the library—listen to how you were just talking about it."

"But you're more important."

He glances down, indecision all over his face, before those gorgeous eyes meet mine again. "That's what I was supposed to say, wasn't it?"

His words hang between us for a long time.

"We said we were putting that behind us," I remind him.

"And we will." He opens his mouth again but cuts off. "We'll figure it out. I promise." He stops me before I can push some more. "And *no*, it won't be because you all uproot your lives for me. I'd love that. Knowing I got to come home to my family, but the guilt would kill me, Mack. The kids love school. Their friends. They need stability."

"They need you."

"I know." His jaw sets. "And I need you all as well. So like I said, we'll figure it out."

I can't lie, I'm relieved that he didn't want to take that option. Sure, leaving the library would have been hard, but I'd do it in a heartbeat. It's the upending Kiera and Van that's the problem. We didn't realize how much more complicated our whole arrangement would be by adding kids to the mix. They were this golden ideal of family life, and while I don't regret them at all, I do wish parenting and life with kids was more transparent.

"What does this all mean?" I ask. "For us?"

"It means … I think it means we'll see. I don't want to jump back into a relationship only for us to end up miserable again. Just … let's try and work it out."

"But no dating anyone else," I hurry to add. "We're going to fix this, and I don't want anyone getting in the way of that."

"Agree." He scowls. "No more Luke."

"He's my friend. That's all it ever was and all it was going to be."

"He wants more."

"I don't think he knows what he wants. I think he wants to settle down, but not necessarily with me. I do hope he finds his person, though, because I like him."

Davey's mouth flattens. "I'm going to have to be okay with that, aren't I?"

"I hope you are." The note in *The Hobbit* shifts through my mind, leaving me uncomfortable for a whole second before it changes. My memory tickles over *Davey* bringing up *The Hobbit. Davey* talking about the dwarves.

Was that a coincidence?

Or … could it have been Davey?

Each note flits through my mind, and this time, I hear them in his voice. With his love behind them.

If that last one was left by him, the whole context changes.

I won't give up.

Wild how something can go from creepy to romantic just based on who it's from.

I smile. "You'll like Luke. And you have nothing to be jealous of. My heart has always been yours."

The relief that crosses his face is something I feel in my bones. "In that case, I'll be friendly."

"Thanks." I stand up and yawn. "We should probably leave it there. That was a whole hell of a lot we covered."

"It was."

I pick up my book and send a cheeky grin his way. "Besides, I have porn waiting for me."

Davey groans, pretending to melt into the couch, while I leave with an "*Oooh, his ravaged hole!*"

I'm not sure what comes next for us, but I know it's leading one way. All this time with winning him over, I'd wanted someone on my side to help us succeed, but turns out the only person I needed was him.

23

Davey

WHEN I WAKE UP IN THE SPARE ROOM TO THE SOUND OF laughter downstairs, I breathe the easiest I have in … fuck. Maybe ever. My good mood lasts the whole morning, through breakfast with the family, joking with Mack and getting the kids ready for school.

If I'm honest, I hadn't realized how heavily this decision has been weighing on me. No matter what I did with the kids or Mack, it always had that tinge of darkness to it that I've never been able to consciously identify. Now, I can. Because looking at them, I know I'll have to leave again, but if I have my way, it'll be the last time. I've never had that freedom before.

I'm cleaning up breakfast from the pancakes that Mack cooked when my phone rings. I snatch it up without checking the caller ID, then have a split second of panic that I've accidentally answered a work call.

"Hello?"

"Hey, I need your kids."

I blink for a second, sure I haven't heard right. Then I pull the phone away, see Art's name, and go back to the call. "I've missed something in this conversation."

He chuckles. "My niblings are coming over tonight for a sleepover, and I thought I could steal Payne's nieces and your kids and make a full event out of it."

My eyes narrow as I fill a pan with water. "And Uncle Art woke up this morning and decided a sleepover sounded like a great idea, did he?"

"Scout's honor."

"Uh-huh."

He huffs. "Fine. I'm trying to give you two some alone time. I'm stealing kids from all over the town to make it happen, so shut up and send your monsters my way."

"Uh, Mr. FBI man who's listening in: he doesn't actually mean *steal*. You can hear him asking for permission here … kinda."

"No one's listening to our calls."

"True. If they were, you would have been arrested a long time ago." I dry my hands and turn toward where I can hear the three of them thudding around upstairs. It's tempting to take Art up on his offer. He's great with his niblings, and I know he'd look after Kiera and Van as fiercely as he does them—he's a kid around grown-ups and a mature grown-up around kids.

Plus, it gives me free time with Mack. Maybe even enough to take him on a date.

"What are you going to do with them?"

"Bake, play dress-ups, then watch a movie until they crash from their sugar high."

"Sounds well thought-out."

"Not my first rodeo."

I move the phone to my other ear. "Does this mean I'll finally get to find out where you live?"

"Nope. We're invading Joey's place for the night. He's only got the lease until right after Christmas, and then he'll be moving in with me, so we might as well make use of it while we can."

"And you're going to have them for the whole night? Six kids?"

"And because you don't think I can, I will. I don't see how six is any different to two."

Oh, that naive man. "I'll keep my phone on."

Kiera and Van are herded into the kitchen by Mack.

"Hey," I say, holding my phone away from my ear. "Who wants a sleepover with Uncle Art?"

"Ohhh, I do!" Kiera shouts.

"Me. Van, do. Van sleepover."

"All yours," I tell him as Mack makes *what the fuck* eyes over the kids' heads.

I hang up the phone and step closer to him as Kiera tries to stuff her lunch box into her bag. "I thought, maybe, if you're free …"

"Yeah?"

"Wanna go on a date with me?"

Mack sucks in a breath, and it's a challenge not to kiss him. My fingers brush the side of his hand before he turns it, grabs mine, then lifts it and presses a kiss to my knuckles. "What do you have in mind? Dinner? A movie?"

"I don't know yet. No movie—I want to do something where we can actually hang out again. Chat. Have fun …"

His eyes have lost that sadness they've been clinging to for so long. "I can't wait to see what you come up with."

"Great." Then because I can't stop myself, I lean in and kiss him on the cheek. "Come on, kids, let's get a move on!"

Turning my focus to them stops me fixating on the sweet little smile that I leave on Mack's face.

The whole time he's working, I'm googling fun things to do in Kilborough on a date. There's the usual dinner, walk along the boardwalk, get extreme at Killer Adventures—hey, go, Payne!—and axe throwing at Killer Brew. Scrolling … scrolling … scrolling …

Wait.

On Friday nights, one of the businesses that belong to the Kil Pen ecosystem has a paint and sip night. I look through the booking form and find platter selections, drinks packages, and canvas size choices. From what I can tell, we paint each other while we eat dinner and drink, and then we get to take the "masterpieces" home with us.

Well, fuck. It'll be nothing if not amusing.

I book a "couple's night out" and then hope like hell Mack's into it.

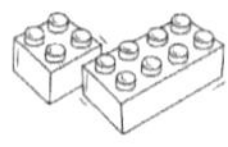

"Do you think this counts as child abuse?" Mack mutters after dropping Kiera and Van off. They were so excited to be spending the night with Uncles Art and Joey and all their "friends." Who they've only met a handful of times, but I wasn't about to point that out to them.

"No, forcing our children to spend time with Art isn't child abuse." I head toward Kil Pen. "Besides, we didn't force anything. If we didn't have the child lock on, they would have launched themselves out of the car before I even got us into the driveway."

He sighs. "I know. I worry."

"Of course you do. But while Art acts like an idiot most of the time, you know he's good with kids."

Mack relaxes. "You're right."

"Always am."

"So where are we going?"

"You just need to wait and see."

"I'm waiting and seeing," he says, peering out the window.

It doesn't take us long to get there. Thankfully, with summer and Halloween over, the main tourist season has wound down, and it's late enough that most of the businesses have closed.

"What's this?" Mack asks as I pull up.

I jump out of the car and round it to open his door, then take his hand. Mack's answering smile is almost shy.

"It's either going to be the best or worst date we've ever had."

"I dunno, you remember the weekend we spent in Boston?"

Mack had ended up with the stomach flu, and we spent the whole trip in our hotel room. "Eh. It was shitty for you, but I at least got to look after you."

"Pun intended?" he grumbles.

"Come on. Just try to keep an open mind."

The look he gives me does not fill me with confidence that he's doing that. So I'll have to stay upbeat for the both of us.

It's a small restaurant, lots of cement tabletops, lights on strings, and exposed steel beams on the ceiling. There's a line of yellow, orange, and green glass bottles along one windowsill and black-and-white framed photos on the far wall.

Candles sit in the middle of all the tables and across the counter, and every table has a small easel on either side.

"Huh" is all Mack says.

"Evening. Who do we have here?" the young waitress asks, pulling out a tablet.

"The booking is under Eiser."

"Got it. I've set the lovebird seat up for you. This way."

She leads us to a spot in the back. It has two deep chairs that feel like a hug and a wide cement table between them.

"You can get started creating art whenever you like, and I'll be out with drinks and food soon."

Mack's gaze roams from her to the canvas and then over to me. "We're painting?"

I laugh at the way his voice squeaks higher. "Sure are. Portraits of each other."

"You're kidding me."

I squeeze some paint out onto the dish, having no clue what I'm doing but trying to look confident about it anyway. "The night is what we make it."

He still looks torn, but his desire for this to go well wins out. "Fine. But I hope you know it's going to be bad."

"Baby, I'm counting on it."

The soft redness that creeps up Mack's cheeks fills me with the urge to lean over the table and kiss him. But that's not what tonight is about. Tonight is for us to reconnect, and dammit, I'm going to make it happen.

"Read any more of that book today?"

He almost drops the black tube of paint he's wrestling with. "Stop trying to embarrass me."

"I'm not. I'm genuinely interested."

His eyes narrow as he fills the dish with paint and picks up a brush. "Might have finished it."

"Oh, really?"

"And started on the second."

I want to laugh so bad, but I hold back. "Enjoying them, huh?"

"Yes, but it's not what you think! The plot is really good."

"You're reading for the plot. Got it."

"I *am*."

I pretend to act skeptical, but Mack's always loved fantasy-type books. The fact he was able to finish it in one night is impressive. "Told Beau you're reading it yet?"

He shakes his head, studying me for a moment before he starts to paint. "Too awkward. Don't think I will."

"Eh, I'm just glad you're enjoying it again."

"What about you? Built anything new?"

"Hmm …" I concentrate on getting Mack's face shape right while I work through how it felt in my shed the other day. "I haven't."

"Why not?"

"Well, I wanted to the other day, but when I went out there … I dunno, Mack. It didn't feel right. That room felt like it was taking me away from you all, and I've done that more than enough."

His jaw tics, and at first, I think he's going to agree with me, but he changes course. "You could try building something in the house?"

"With Kiera and Van around?"

"They love doing it with you." He pauses. "Maybe we could go home and build something together?"

"Like the Millennium Falcon you broke?"

"Hey, I said I was sorry!" His blush has started to come back, and it's so fucking adorable. "And I don't think I'm up to something like that."

"Relax. It would take way too long anyway. That might be a project for when I'm home … more …" I almost say *permanently*, but I don't want to put that in his head yet.

"You were serious then?" he whispers. "About figuring something out."

"I'm serious about wanting to try."

His sweet blue eyes meet mine, and they're filled with so much hope it takes my breath away. "Do you think your job would let you have more time working from home?"

No. They couldn't even give me this one. If they had, I probably wouldn't be ready to jump ship on them. They've given me a lot of good years, but when it comes right down to it, they're a big company, and I'm one person. One person who's easy enough to replace. "I can only ask, right?"

Thankfully, conversation steers away from work. Mack fills me in on the gossip from the library, and I tell him about gossip from school pickup. We alternate painting and eating, and painting and drinking, and for the first time in so long, our conversation doesn't revolve around the kids or have that added tension hanging over it.

"Okay, I'm done," I tell him. It's not a masterpiece, but it turned out better than I thought it would. At least it sort of vaguely looks like a badly painted version of him. His hair, skin, and eyes are all remotely the same color.

"Ah …" His eyes swing from his painting to me, and he exposes his teeth. "I think I'm … done."

"I'll go first." I turn the picture around, trying not to laugh, and the look that crosses his face is a mixture of horror and amusement.

"That's actually not terrible," he says, choking on his words. "I'm not sure *what* it is, but it's *not* terrible."

"Okay, Michelangelo. Your turn."

He snatches up the canvas before I can and clutches it in front of his chest. "It needs time to, uh, dry."

"Bullshit." I make a gimme motion with my hands. "Show me."

Mack's shoulders are already shaking with silent laughter as he turns the canvas and whispers, "I'm so sorry."

It's an assault on my vision. The zigzags of my curls, how he's painted my skin so dark I'm the wrong ethnicity altogether, and he's had to make my freckles yellow to stand out, my football-shaped skull, or how my eyes are so misaligned one of them is almost touching my mouth.

Mack and I stare at each other. Then at Franken-Davey. Then back to each other again.

The laugh that tears from me sounds like some kind of animal call, and Mack follows right behind me.

We laugh until my stomach hurts, and then we laugh some more.

24

Mack

I'm more than a little tipsy and happy by the time we get home. Davey's driving, so he only had two, but the combination of my lack of artistic skills and the good food made the beers slide down too easily.

Tonight was like old times.

As soon as we step inside, he kicks off his boots, and I follow before we hang our coats in the hall cupboard. The heat was left on, so it's not too bad inside, but it's going to take a minute for my face to thaw out.

"Thanks for tonight," I say, dopey grin stretched wide. "You've still got it."

"My date game is strong."

"Always was." I glance up to find him blatantly checking me out. There's something about the way his dark eyes light up when they're running over me that makes me want to strip off and ask for more.

Feeling daring, I ask, "Hey, remember after our first-ever date?"

A corner of his lips kicks up. "When you blew me in the car because you were too scared to come inside?"

"It was our first date. And you lived with your parents."

"*Temporarily*." He looks like he's trying not to laugh. "I'd just graduated and was working out what was next."

I shrug, feeling cocky. "Next was me."

"It definitely was." He pinches the front of my sweater and tugs me closer. "It was never supposed to be."

"What do you mean?"

"I had this whole idea. I'd get a job, move away, maybe settle down in my midthirties."

"What happened to those big fancy plans?"

"I met you." Davey's gaze is filled with the same affection squeezing my heart. "This man I thought I'd go out with one time, hopefully get in his pants, then leave behind the second I was out of here."

"But you went and fell in love with me instead."

There's no regret, no bitterness. None of those negative emotions can touch us tonight. "Almost immediately."

"What was it?" I have the guts to ask. I'll be thanking the alcohol for all these questions later. "There are plenty of other men out there. I'm sure you've met loads of great ones while traveling all the time."

"I've met some really, really great people."

"Then …"

"They're just people. It's hard to pinpoint what it is I love about you because it's not one thing. It's not your eyes. Or your laugh. Or the way you're so … so … *earnest* sometimes.

One of those things without the rest isn't you." Davey's fingers trail over the back of my hand. "It's the way these fingers grip the books you read." Slide along my forearm. "And how you hold our babies in these arms." He reaches my neck. "The way you go so red, right here, when you get embarrassed about the most ridiculous things." Both hands cup my jaw. "It's your eyes saying what your mouth can't, and it's the truly filthy things you sometimes let slip past your lips …" The raw emotion in his tone is something I've yearned for every year since I lost it.

I tell myself I'm not going to cry because that would be stupid, but Davey goes all out of focus anyway. The moment hovers so painfully tight with tension between us, and I know I shouldn't. I know we're working through things, don't want to move too fast, blah, blah, blah.

But I defy anyone to hear those things said about them and not be hungry for the one saying them.

Then Davey's eyes sharpen. The sweet awe disappears, and the hunger in my gut is mirrored back at me.

"You know what? Fuck it."

Our mouths crash together, lips part, teeth clashing and tongues meeting. The burning in my soul is impossible to ignore, and all I want and need right now is Davey.

I grope at his shoulders, bodies fused together as I fit one hand between us to get to work on his buttons. The clothes need to go. Fucking winter. Fucking layers.

One of Davey's large hands is set possessively on my lower back while he tugs up the side of my sweater with his other.

"Need," he grunts into my mouth. "Off. Now."

"Then we have to stop kissing," I manage to get out as he does the complete opposite. Talking with another mouth fused to yours isn't the easiest, but I don't want him to go anywhere either.

His frustrated growl is music to my ears as his mouth breaks away, but like he changes his mind at the last minute, he redirects to my neck.

The sensitive skin sends ripples through me as he sucks on the spot that drives me wild. He still knows my body. And I still know his.

I reach the bottom button and push the shirt from his shoulders. The fucking thermal is still between me and skin, and I'm not above playing dirty. My thigh slots perfectly between his legs, and he grinds his hard-on into it in response.

"*Fuuuuck*, Mack."

"Need you naked." I really turn on the begging. "Please."

He shoves away from me, rips the undershirt over his head, then roughly drags my sweater off me. We're separated for a handful of seconds before we're both shirtless, but it's too many.

Davey kisses me so hard I stumble backward and into the wall. His hands work open the front of my pants, and he yanks them down. "Can't wait. Need you now."

"I always need you," I promise him.

"Turn around."

I do as I'm told, gripping the wall for support, and then Davey's hands close over my ass cheeks and spread them apart. He lands spit right on my hole and pushes a finger in.

The stretch sends bubbles of lust to my head. It's been too long since he's been inside me, and the dildo that's kept me company all these years can only do so much. It's never hit that deep ache like he does.

"That's it, baby, open for me." His voice is a barely

contained rasp. "You've always been so good at taking my cock."

"My body knows what it needs."

He presses another finger in. My grip on the wall tightens briefly, but we've done this so many times, in so many positions and places and ways, that preparing for him comes naturally to me. As easily as breathing.

He leaves my ass for a second, and I glance back over my shoulder to find him freeing his own cock and shoving his pants down his thighs. I've missed his cock so much. The curve, his scent, the way his tip feels under my tongue. I'm torn between the need to feel him stretching my lips or stretching my ass.

More spit, and then he fills me with three fingers this time, giving me time to adjust as he slowly strokes himself.

"You want this, don't you?"

"Yes," I beg.

When he goes back to stretching me, he brushes my prostate, increasing my horniness with every pass.

I'm so damn obsessed. So needy. A shiver rakes my limbs.

"You want a taste," he whispers.

"Please."

"Get on your knees."

I drop as soon as his fingers are clear of me, and Davey holds himself steady while I lean forward eagerly and suck him down.

"You haven't fucked anyone else since me," he says, and I hum my agreement around his length.

"And I haven't fucked anyone since you. You trust me, don't you?"

I nod. If there's anyone I trust, it's him.

"Then get me nice and wet, baby. That's it … we're not stopping for supplies, and I don't want to hurt you."

My eyes roll back. Need surging back hard and fast. I double down on my efforts until his dick is drenched in my saliva, and then he hauls me to my feet.

I grip the wall, Davey steps up behind me, and then his cock presses against my ass.

He pushes forward, and I relax into it, body stretching to let him inside. It's been too long since I felt this full, and I don't just mean my ass. Being like this, with Davey, it's a rightness I'll never be able to explain in my life. He's my person. And I'm his. The time apart doesn't matter when I'm so sure that the universe will always bring us back together. Like this. Over and over for forever.

With one last, full thrust, he buries his cock inside me, and we both let out twin sighs. My pants are still binding my legs, and his are doing the same, but they're easy to ignore when he rolls his hips, thrusting inside me, nose by my ear and hands on my pecs.

"How did I go without you for so long?" he asks.

"Doesn't matter. Nothing matters. Just fuck me. Hard, fast, slow, deep. I don't care."

We fuck against the wall for what feels like an hour. His hands explore my body, and we kiss over my shoulder, and I strangle my cock in a vise every time I get too close to the edge.

He does exactly what I said. Fucks me hard and fast. Then deep and slow. He leans back to watch as he draws himself teasingly out to the tip and then slams home again. The only time we pause is for him to add more spit, to the point I feel sticky and used and so, so good.

My balls are sitting high and tight. Waiting for that moment of release. But there's something about tonight that neither of us wants to let go of, and what happens next is still a possibility, but this moment is so perfect I want it to go on forever.

This is what life's about. Davey and Mack. Me and him. Two men, meant to be.

My legs are straining with the effort of holding myself upright, arm against the wall getting kind of numb as my ass takes a beating.

Davey's heavy breaths get louder as his hands slide back up to my pecs. Each pass of his thumb over my nipple is almost too much.

"Don't want this to end," he says, biting my shoulder.

"Me neither."

"But I'm gonna come. So close."

"Okay." I'm not sure if I'm even making words at this point. "Do it. Fill me up."

He groans deeply, then pulls back, sets his hands on my hips, and pounds his way toward the end. My cock is pure relief when I finally touch it and jerk myself off.

I'm building closer, closer, the ache in my balls reaching that addictive high of my orgasm, and right as it hits me, a wave of emotion follows behind it.

"I love you so much," I gasp out as my cum hits the wall, and Davey's cry behind me lets me know he's followed me over.

I'm done first, catching my breath, sweat cooling against my skin as he milks the last drops of cum into me. Then, he melts against my back. He softly kisses his way up my neck until his head rests against mine.

"I love you too, Mack. Never stopped. Never will."

When he slips out, I pull up my pants, then take his hand. "Come on."

"Where are we going?"

"To shower so you can clean me up, then to bed. Our bed. Where you belong."

Tears spill onto Davey's cheeks, and mine spring up instantly. He pulls me into his arms, and we stand there together, and I think I'm sobbing, and he's sobbing, but for once, there's nothing sad about it. I'm just so fucking relieved.

25

Davey

Two weeks. Mack and the kids both finish up school and work at the end of this week, meaning we're going to have a lot of time together. The problem is, two weeks seems like way too short a time.

Which is hilarious when this is the usual amount of time I get to spend with them.

How did I ever think that was enough?

My departure is looming over my head. Sure, banking all of this leave to use at once was a great idea, but all it's done is shown me what I was missing. Made me want for things I was better off not wanting, especially when I can't find an out.

Even Art's contacts were quiet. He's going to try again in the new year, but I'd be lying if I said that I wasn't worried about going back to work and getting complacent again. My job is the type of job people don't resign from.

I pull my laptop out and hole up at the table, feeling so remarkably at home. I've never let myself get this way before, always knowing how soon I need to leave again, but I'm going to fight tooth and nail to stop from going this time.

All it would take is another job.

On a whim, and almost scared to do it, I pull up our budget and then … delete my salary off it. I stare at the glaring red numbers, faced with the reality of what quitting means. We're either paying the mortgage or paying for Kiera and Van's schooling and groceries. We have no extra for college. Nothing to cover insurance, let alone come close to the health plan I'm on at work.

Dates like the other night? Forget it.

It's so tempting—and that temptation is becoming worse every day—to send in my resignation and be done with it. But if that happens, this is the result.

There's no way Mack and I could possibly be happy living one bill away from losing everything. Sure, we have savings set aside now, but dipping into that is a slippery slope to fore-closure and bankruptcy.

I cup my hands and scream into them, wanting this to be fucking easy for once. We've done hard. We've paid our fucking dues. When does this end?

I'm torturing myself going over it again and again. Nothing has changed. My options haven't shifted. The time of year has me kneecapped by how much I can achieve, and at this rate, I'll be driving back to work in two weeks.

I can do it. I can get through, knowing that a solution is coming.

Except nothing has jumped out at you before.

I flip off the negative voice, snap my laptop shut, then snatch up my keys and head into town. For once, I don't want to talk to someone. I want to buy a coffee to keep my hands warm, then take the longest walk along the boardwalk imaginable.

I pull up at Killer Brew and order, then hang back in the chilly air and wait. It's as I'm waiting that a familiar face approaches, and every nerve in my body makes me want to turn away and pretend I haven't seen him.

But I don't.

For Mack.

If he says Luke is okay, I have to trust him.

Luke orders, cheeks as slapped red as his hair, and it's not until he steps away that he notices me. That same friendly smile he was wearing the day he came to the house crosses his face, and the suspicious side of me tries to see through the bullshit.

"Davey, right?" he asks, approaching. I have to give it to him: it takes some serious confidence to approach the ex-husband of the man you kissed two weeks ago. He points at his chest. "Luke."

"I know."

"Ah." His smile falters. "If it helps, all he ever did was talk about you."

That *does* help chip away at my dislike of him. "It does. Slightly."

Luke laughs and ducks his chin into his scarf. "You can't blame me for trying. Mack's a great guy, and I want to settle down. But I know he's not my guy. I just want you to know that you won't get any problems from me—even if you didn't already own Mack's whole heart."

"Thanks." I hesitate, then hold out my hand. Luke shakes it. "I appreciate you saying that."

He shrugs, hands back in his pockets. "Yeah, I don't like

the home-wrecker thing some people are into. I like this town. I want to make some friends, maybe find a guy of my own, build a life here, you know? I don't want issues with anyone."

"If you're true to your word, then you won't have issues with me."

"Thanks." He chews the inside of his lip. "Are you … are you going to hate if Mack and I are friends?"

My automatic answer is *fuck yes, stay away from him,* but I swallow it down. "It will be weird, but I'll get used to it. I trust him completely. And you say you won't be an issue, so …"

His sigh is caught by the breeze. "That means a lot. I've been here a year and only really know people in passing. Ford and Orson are always great to hang out with, and I have a couple of friends from work."

"Where do you work?"

"Up at Kil Pen. Do tours and stuff. It's been great."

"Hmm …" My gaze drifts to where I can make out a corner of it from behind Killer Brew. "Quiet time of year now, isn't it?"

"Yep. Thankfully I'm one of their full-time staff, but there are a fair few people we said goodbye to in early November. So that part sucks."

"I bet."

My coffee is called, which gets me out of continuing the forced conversation. "Well, I'll see you around."

Surprisingly, I don't completely dread that idea.

My walk takes me around the lake and back again. I'm moving enough that it keeps the cold away, even if my coffee doesn't agree, and the mindless walking does the trick of easing my frustration.

Or maybe that was the conversation with Luke. No idea.

On my way back to the car, I find myself detouring away

from the water and toward the large building a block away. It's all red brick with a short spire on one side that holds a large clock face.

I can see why Mack loves it here. There's a park across the road, and every time I've been here recently, I can see us spending the morning with Kiera and Van at the park before picking out a book on the way home.

Hell, maybe Mack can pick out some more sexy books too. I wouldn't be opposed to reading those to him before bedtime.

My footsteps slow as I reach the doors and check inside to make sure he isn't at his desk. It's clear, so I tilt my head down and walk quickly, ducking down the usual aisle and following my path toward the back where the fiction books are.

For something so popular, *The Hobbit* mustn't be a book many people read because it's sitting right where it normally is.

I pull it out and then realize I have no fucking clue what to write this time.

My Hobbit knowledge only goes so far, and I don't care what Mack says: this book is boring as fuck. I've never been able to get past the front page. Thank you, Google.

"I knew it was you."

"Argh." I jump and drop the book, the hard corner smashing into my foot. Pain shoots up my leg, and I struggle to hold back the curse that tries to slip out.

"Shit, I'm sorry," Mack says, stooping to pick it up.

"I'm okay," I grit out.

Mack laughs. "I was talking to the book."

"There is no way that's true."

He slides *The Hobbit* back onto the shelf and turns sympathetic eyes on me. "You okay?"

"Fine. It was just … sudden. I guess."

"Right."

I shake my foot out for emphasis, and then his words catch up with me. "What do you mean, you knew?"

He leans back against the shelf. "At first, I thought it might have been Luke leaving me the notes. He likes the book, and he had visited when I found those first two left for me."

"Of course he had," I mutter.

"But the next one didn't sound like him. Then when you mentioned it the other night, I checked the handwriting again …" His smile starts out slow and builds. "You've never even watched the movies."

It's my turn to act cocky. "What do you think I've been doing while you were working?"

"You watched them?"

"Well, I haven't been sitting around doing nothing, have I?"

He watches me for a moment. "Which ones?"

"Which what?"

"Movies. Which ones have you watched? Did you do the series as well?"

"Ah … series?"

"Yeah, there's a TV series."

Of fucking course there is. "I watched *The Hobbit*. And the two after. You're telling me there's a *series* too?"

"Wait. You skipped *Lord of the Rings*?"

I do not like where this is going. "Umm … if you promise not to ask me for any of the details … no?"

"You did!"

"I thought there was just *The Hobbit*! They already squeezed three movies out of the one book. What else could they have done?"

He sighs and steps closer, then pulls out one … two …

three heavy books. "These are the Lord of the Rings. Three books, three movies. The director's cut versions are over three hours long. And the effects? They were unmatched in those days. Legolas, Gandalf, and Bilbo are both in this trilogy too and—"

My hand comes down over his mouth. "Slow down there, nerd." His eyes light up. "What I'm hearing is that I'm not nearly caught up enough and we have a movie marathon in our future."

He snatches my hand away. "We can watch the first on Saturday night when the kids are in bed. Then Sunday morning, your parents always want to take them for a couple of hours, so we can watch the second, and then we'll wrap up the third on Sunday night. It'll be perfect."

And maybe I'm feeling sentimental, or slightly guilty over having to leave again soon, or I've just forgotten how much these things are so not *my* thing, but I agree.

The lengths I'll go to just to spend time with him.

"You're letting me pick the snacks."

DMC GROUP CHAT

Mack: I get the feeling none of you are crossing your fingers for a white Christmas like I asked, and I'm going to need you to do that a little harder.

Art: No matter how much you try, you can't actually make it snow. You know that, right?

Mack: Can and will. I'll hunt Jack Frost down myself if I have to.

Griff: Can I come too? He sounds hot.

Payne: A fictional, not at all real, entity sounds hot?

Griff: I bet he'd be the kind to ruin you for anyone else and not call back in the morning.

Orson: Yeah, I doubt he'd ruin anything judging by how my body reacts to being in the snow.

Art: Are we sure the snow is the reason for that issue?

Orson: Either that, or my balls never dropped.

Payne: Art's the only one with that issue.

Art: Fuck you, my balls are exactly where they're supposed to be.

Art: In Joey's mouth.

Keller: You set him up for that one.

26

Mack

"THANKS FOR DOING THIS," I SAY. "I TOLD DAVEY I HAD AN overtime shift today, so we'll have to be quick." Technically, this was supposed to be the kids' and my first day off for winter break, but I needed to sneak away.

Davey's mom smiles over the counter at me. She has the same dark freckles over her nose that he does and the same wild black curls. "This is so romantic, Mack. You really do have the biggest heart of anyone I know."

"Well, Davey deserves the world. He makes it easy to be."

She gives me that same loving, slightly guilty look she's worn around me since the divorce. "It still hurts every day that you didn't work out."

We're going to though. I don't tell her that because I don't want to get anyone's hopes up, not even mine, but I can feel the certainty in my bones. I'm not going to give up. If we have to go back to him traveling all the time, at least I'll do that knowing what it was like in the same position, but without being able to call him mine. That should help me get through. Hopefully.

I play with my fingers as I answer her. "Even if I can't have him, I *want* to go on loving him forever. No matter what."

She hiccups a sob before pulling herself together. "And you'll always be our son. No matter what."

"Thank you." Davey's parents welcoming me so easily was one of my favorite things about marrying him. Mom and Dad had me later in life, and while we all loved each other, we were never the closest of families. It's one of the reasons I suggested Davey keep living with us; married or not, I want the kids to grow up knowing that we're always there for them.

"Well, then," I say, wanting to steer this conversation away from tears since I'm all dried out of those. "Where do we start?"

Mary helps me gather ingredients and props up the handwritten instructions. "It was what I could remember, so we might need to play with measurements until we get it right."

"I'm game for that. There's a whole four hours until I have to get back for him to pick me up."

"Won't he notice when you aren't paid any extra?"

I pull out a pan and set it on the stove. "That won't be until after Christmas, and I will have told him before then. I don't keep secrets from Davey."

"You need to stop that."

"Stop what?"

"Being such a good person. You could at least have a tiny bit of asshole in you so I could be like *there, that's why my son walked away from the best man he's ever known*, but no. You keep being perfect."

"But … I'm not." I turn and look at her, genuinely upset she's so hard on him. "You do know it was me who suggested the divorce, right?"

"Because he wouldn't quit his job."

And as she says those words, it sinks in that those weren't our only issues. If I'm considering building our life back to what it was, his work and all, that proves it wasn't really about that. "That's the reason I used, but honestly, I think it was easier to blame him than look at myself."

"What do you mean?"

It's hard to talk about, but I owe it to him. "There was a lot going on back then. Van was a baby, and he was a lot to deal with. Kiera wasn't exactly easy. And all I saw was Davey getting to have two whole weeks to himself. Getting to have his own life. Having a successful career and friends, and I … everything felt so dark. I didn't talk to him about any of it, and when I think about it now, that was unfair to him. He did everything when he was home, including work, and he missed so much when he was gone. He was my only anchor when everything got hard, and he wasn't there when I needed him."

"I know, honey, but—"

I shake my head quickly. "I shouldn't need him. That's my point. You don't stay with someone because you need them; you stay with them because you want them. Because they make your life better. We weren't making each other's lives better then, and it was my fault. I'd get sulky when he talked about work, so he stopped. I had nothing of my own. Nothing but him and the kids. And that's not healthy."

Her mouth tightens. "That's not all on you."

"Maybe not, but I was so focused on resenting him that I forgot to be grateful for everything I did have because of him. He missed huge parts of the kids growing up so I got to experience it. He worked so hard so I didn't have to work at all. He was always the one giving, and I was always the one taking." I nod to the recipe. "I'm not doing that anymore. Now, I'm focusing on my life. On what makes me happy and a whole person, and maybe if I do that, I'll be able to appreciate the things that make Davey a whole person too."

"Mack …" She pulls me into a Mom-swamping hug, squeezing me as hard as her tiny arms can handle. The hug lasts longer than it should, but I know she's trying not to cry, so I don't mention anything. When she pulls away, some of the usual guilt is gone from her stare. "I really do love my son. I know I'm hard on him sometimes, but—"

"Sounds like we all are."

"Ah. Shit."

"Can't change that now though. All we can do is figure out this recipe while I get his LEGO rebuilt and we cross fingers like hell that it snows on Christmas. He leaves again soon, and I want to make sure he enjoys every last day home with us before he goes again."

She opens her mouth to say something when the front door opening makes us freeze.

"Mom? You home?"

Davey.

I snatch the recipe from the counter and do a panicked spin for a hiding space before ducking into the pantry. It's one of those open ones with no door, but unless he comes right around the corner and into the kitchen, he won't see me.

Maybe.

Fuck.

I told him I was at work, so if he finds me here, I'm going to have to explain.

Mary waves at me to get down, so I crouch, then jump as she throws a dish towel over my head.

We exchange silent, frantic *what the fuck* gestures before she straightens and plasters a smile onto her face. Mary disappears from sight, and I crouch there, heart thumping, with an incessant urge to pee.

"Hello, my munchkins," she says, and Kiera and Van both answer her.

"We're heading down to the park," Davey says. "Thought Grandma might want to join us."

"Oh, baby, I would, but I … I have so much cleaning to do … And …"

I remember all the ingredients scattered around the kitchen and facepalm.

"What are you cooking?" he asks.

"Just lunch. Nothing fun. Nothing special. Might want to skip the park—it's freezing out there. Probably better to hole up at home with a movie until you have to pick Mack up."

"He told you he picked up a shift?"

"Yeah, we talked. Umm, on the phone. This morning."

"Okay." There's a light scuffling. "Looks like it's just us, kids."

"Fine …" Kiera says.

"Wow, don't sound too excited."

"Why did Dad have to work? We wanted both of you to take us. It's not fair."

With one little sentence, the menace breaks my heart in half. I'm about to pop out of my terrible hiding space and be all, "Surprise, we can," when Davey gets in first.

"You're allowed to be disappointed when something doesn't work out, but it's up to you where we go from here. The three of us can try to have fun going down the icy-cold slide, or we can miss out completely because we want to be sad about something we can't change instead."

She takes a minute to think, and so do I. Maybe if my parents had taught me that lesson when I was younger, we never would have gotten into this mess in the first place. Or maybe I would have fucked it all up anyway. Either way, I'm learning. And Davey might only get to parent half the time I do, but he's just taught me something about it anyway.

It's okay for the kids to feel disappointed. When he leaves, it's okay for them to feel sad. But it's not okay for me to let them wallow in their feelings because I'm stuck in mine. We need to make the choice. My life doesn't have to stop when he's not here.

"Can we get ice cream?" Kiera asks with all the rationalizing skill a kid needs.

"Me ice cream. Me ice cream. Van ice cream too."

I have to choke down my laugh as Davey answers in a long-suffering voice. "I guess we're getting ice cream. In winter. At the freezing cold park."

"Don't leave them out in the weather too long," Mary calls, and judging by the way her volume increases, they must be leaving.

I don't hear what else is said, but I sink down onto the floor with relief that I wasn't found.

When she comes back, my own relief is mirrored on her face. "That was close."

"Sure was." I climb to my feet and return to the kitchen, propping the recipe back up again.

"I dunno, Davey's going to spoil those two," she says. "Gives them everything they want."

I think of the gentle way he corrected Kiera's thoughts and smile to myself. "Maybe. But he's giving them what they need too." I point at the recipe. "So we're doing the same for him. Back to this. We have three and a half hours left, and I don't think I'll be able to lie about overtime again. Doing it once was hard enough."

Mary ties back her hair, determination settling on her face. "Let's do it, then."

27

Davey

Something's going on. All weekend, Mack keeps needing to duck out to "appointments" or to "catch up with a friend," and given it's only days until Christmas, something isn't adding up. If he was ducking out to pick up Christmas gifts, I'd get it, but I've already got those organized.

I'd assumed since this is the two-week block that we always have together that we'd be spending whatever time we could in each other's company. Maybe that was short-sighted of me. Of course he has his own life and his own friends, and it's not fair of me to expect him to put an end to all of that just to hang out with me.

Especially since the time we have together is perfect.

We're still sharing our bed, I still get to wake up to that gorgeous sleepy face—even if Van is wedged in between us. There hasn't been any more sex, which is probably a good thing since it was so intense and raw last time that I can't get through that again with everything still so uncertain between us.

There has been kissing though. The type of kissing that makes me feel young again. From the sort that lingers that moment too long to be friendly, nothing else touching between us, to the quick slip of the tongue, to the bold desperateness that flares up between us before one of us remembers to stop. It always leaves me breathless and my gut a knotted mess in the best possible way.

While I appreciate that he let me sleep in this morning, I don't want to wake up without him beside me.

I creep up behind him in the kitchen and wrap my arms around his waist. Mack immediately melts into me, and I can't stop from leaving a lingering kiss on his neck. Right on that spot where his scent is heaviest and gets a sharp inhale from him every time.

"Tell me you don't have plans today?"

The guilty look he throws me over his shoulder is the only answer I need. And honestly, it annoys me a bit.

I step away with a sigh. "Is it at least something I can do with you?"

Mack groans. "Not this time. I have, uh … Ford's got this thing. He needs help with."

"And I can't help because …"

"It's … private! Very private. I've been sworn to secrecy, or I'd totally tell you."

"Husbands don't keep secrets."

"But we're not husbands."

The truth stretches out between us. He's right. Obviously. Doesn't stop from making me want to punch something. Our whole situation is fucked-up, and it's the waiting to be able to do something about it that has me more frustrated than anything.

It's not Mack's fault.

Not spending time with me is though.

So is throwing the fact that we're not actually together back in my face. I have no right to feel hurt. I agreed to it all just the same as he did. We were idiots, obviously, and since we worked that out, we've been honest about where we stand and what we want.

Except for these fucking disappearances.

Following my husband—*ex*, sorry, Mack—wasn't on my list of things to do today, but I'm curious. So curious. I also know how fucked-up it is to be thinking like that, so I swallow my pride and stamp down that need to make Mack think I'm okay always and ask, "Are you seeing Luke?"

I hate how defeated my voice comes out, but I don't know why else he'd be sneaking around.

Mack's head snaps my way, and the shock reflected on it helps ease my jealous suspicion. "No. I'd tell you if I was. I promise."

He doesn't need to promise because I'd believe him without it. "Okay, but I have to be honest here; you sneaking off has me asking questions."

Mack drops his head onto my shoulder. "There's no one else, I already agreed to that. So can you please, *please* try to trust me and know that I wouldn't voluntarily be spending time away from you if I didn't need to and just stop asking questions?"

"Stop asking questions?" I almost laugh until Mack looks up and I catch how earnest those blue eyes look. "Don't give me that look."

"*Pleeease?*"

"No questions asked, huh?"

"It would be helpful."

I don't point out how impossible a request like that actually is, but on the other hand, he shouldn't have to ask me to trust him. When it comes right down to it, Mack is one of the most trustworthy people I know. It's my own insecurities—and probably fear that I might lose him again—coming through.

"Fine. No questions. Disappear when you need to, and I'll look the other way."

I'm rewarded with a kiss. One of those closed-mouthed, too-long, gut-swooping kisses.

My hand finds his lower back, urging him closer, and we break off before things go further, but he doesn't back away. His eyes drop closed as his forehead rests against mine.

I linger in the moment for a second before I step away. "I need a promise from you," I say.

"What is it?"

"I'll keep quiet, but you have to promise not to sneak away tomorrow night. We've already promised the kids we'll take them to the fair together, and I'm not compromising on that."

"Agreed. I've been looking forward to it all week."

I wave a hand toward the door. "Go on, then. Go and help Ford."

"Don't you want me to clean up breakfast?"

"Nope. The sooner you go, the sooner you can be back home with us. The kids want to play board games later."

"That went terribly last time."

"It did. And I'm sure it will again. Which is why I'm not going through it solo."

He laughs and slaps me on the ass as he passes. "It could be payback for all the times I have."

"Low blow."

"Hey, I said I'd move on; I didn't say I'd forget. You still owe me a lot of tantrums before we're even."

There's a small part of me that's worried he's doing that joking-but-serious thing. Until he winks. And in that one tiny action, I know without a doubt that we're going to be okay.

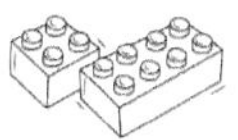

ERIC CALLS PARTWAY THROUGH OUR BOARD GAME, AND MACK clocks his name at the same time as I do. With a deep breath, I silence the call, curious but not enough to put an end to the game.

Mack nudges my phone in my direction. "Better see what he wants."

"We're busy."

"We can wait."

The urge to ignore it and pretend like it never happened is strong. I've gotten so good at not talking about work that having it openly discussed feels like a dirty little secret.

"Before he hangs up."

"Okay. I'll be right back." And hell, if I can get whatever this conversation is done with, it means it won't be hanging over me for the rest of the day.

Unless he suddenly wants me to come back to work tomorrow, then I'll very quickly be out of a job because I won't have any issues with telling him where to stick it. It's hard enough not telling him to fuck off as it is. I've *earned* this time off, dammit.

With the smallest bit of hope that Eric is calling to tell me they don't need me back at work early after all, I answer the call.

"Hey, Eric." I don't mean to sound so short, but I can't even fake a little of my usual professionalism. "I'm in the middle of spending time with my family, so this will have to be quick."

"Of course. We're wrapping up things in the office, so I wanted to call and wish you and Mack happy holidays."

The flicker of hope dies. No Christmas miracles for me. "Right." Too late, I add, "You too."

There's a beat of silence. "I know you're disappointed about the rearrangements, but—"

"It isn't something we'll be discussing today."

"I also wanted to let you know your Christmas bonus should show up today. Congratulations, Davey, you've earned it."

"Thank you. Merry Christmas." I hang up before he gets a chance to reply. I'm sure there'll be a conversation about my rudeness, but that conversation can happen when I'm on the clock. Not now. Not here.

Mack might have been okay with me taking that call, but I'm not. Work already overreaches when it comes to my family time. How many phone calls have I answered over dinner? How many nights did I sit up working on my laptop? The flexibility to be able to work from home is amazing, but it blurs the line between office hours and family time to the point where I always have to be on. Talking to someone in the office as I drive the kids to school or Mack to work is usual. Creating meeting minutes or last-minute updates to a client's package the second the kids are in bed is common.

Once I'm back at work, my professionalism won't be the only conversation we need to have. I'll be drawing clear lines between what's acceptable and what isn't.

I rejoin my family, and the second I'm back cross-legged

on the ground, Van wriggles up into my lap. I hold him close, loving how attached he is, even as my heart breaks over why it might be. Mack is gently teasing Kiera as she lands on a snake during her turn, and then Van rolls the dice, almost knocks the board over, moves Mack's piece instead of his, and shrieks when we try to put it back. Then also shrieks as we try to replace Mack's with the one he's sucking on.

"Van's ruining it!" Kiera pouts.

Van responds by throwing the dice at her head, which immediately has her in tears.

Mack smiles at me over our bawling daughter. I smile at him over where our son is chewing on the side of the board.

"Why do we keep trying to have a games night?" he asks me.

"Because we love it."

He gives me a *you sure about that?* look, but I am. Sure. Because I'll take all the good and bad I can get with these three.

Not even the five-figure bonus I get can change my mind.

28

Mack

THIS WEEK HAS BEEN WAY MORE STRESSFUL THAN IT HAS ANY right to be. Mary and I aren't completely sure we got the recipe right, so I'm relying on Davey's taste buds being shit at this point. His LEGO Millennium Falcon had some, uh, setbacks that involved an old man, an unreliable brake, and a broken wrist. I should be more sorry about Taylor's broken bone than a broken LEGO set, but I'm struggling to find the balance.

Christmas Eve is *two* nights away. Two. I'm running out of time to get everything perfect, even with Ford and his grease monkeys staying back this week to help me. I'd feel guilty about that fact if I wasn't so selfishly determined to make Davey happy and if they all weren't so ridiculously determined to get it done.

"Got everything?" Davey asks, ready to pull the front door closed behind us.

I peck him on the cheek. Even knowing he's back at work in a week, I think I'm the happiest I've been in my life. That might change again when he's actually gone, but for now, I can ignore that and live this, and everything is great. "Think so. We'll buy them fries and corn dogs for dinner."

"That they'll probably throw up after all the rides."

I *do not* want a repeat of last year. Things were tense enough between us before we left the house that losing Van for a solid thirty seconds, having Kiera throw up her food, and then carrying Van out of there screaming has scarred me for tonight. I *want* everything to be perfect, but with my track record so far, "perfect" and "us" don't fit in the same sentence. I'm good at getting things wrong. At putting too much pressure on a moment instead of letting the moments happen.

So I've decided that I'm going to pull up my man panties and take whatever fuckery comes.

The winter fair is held at the sports ground on the edge of town. The fair is expanding, and with it growing that little bit every year, the oval won't be able to hold it soon. I overheard Payne and Art talking about him putting in a proposal to hold it at Killer Adventures.

The more I think about it, the more it would be the perfect location, but given they've only just gotten the place up and running, taking on something this large would have been too much for him.

It's awesome to see him expanding. To see Beau moving in with him. Then there's Griff and Heath, who've made their partnership in Magnolia Ridge official. Ford and Orson, who are looking to open a second garage. Art, who's been prodding Joey to run Killer Brew with him while Joey keeps turning him down. Keller and Will recently settled down. Then me and

Davey. Further behind than we've ever been in terms of our relationship.

And I've never been more positive about the future than I am right now.

Sometimes you have to go back to the foundations and figure out where you went wrong before you can rebuild, and it feels like that's what we're doing. We didn't focus on that the first time around.

The parking situation is a bit of a mess when we arrive, especially with Kiera and Van going wild in the back. The rides are all lit up, music blaring, and even with the droopy gray sky, the whole thing does look magical. I remember coming when I was a kid and thinking it was the most amazing experience ever.

It's not snowing tonight, but it's fucking freezing, and I'm glad we decided to come earlier in the afternoon than usual. Not that it helps. My nose is like ice even under my billions of layers, but Davey's only in jeans, a sweater, and a coat, the smart-ass, and I had to bribe the babies into their puffer jackets. They'd run barefoot through the snow if I didn't stop them.

We line up to grab our tickets, and as soon as we're inside, Kiera can't stop talking. She pulls us from place to place while Van takes a moment to warm up to the overstimulation. The game booths are right at the entrance, with the amusement rides further back. Frozen dirt and gravel on the path crunches under my feet, and I'm glad the kids are holding Davey's hands because my gloved ones are stuffed up under my armpits.

I fucking hate the cold.

I drift a little ways behind them, watching Davey. My gaze travels over his broad shoulders, admiring the way his light brown skin looks against his black coat and curls. How tall he is compared to Kiera and the easy way he has Van tucked up in one arm.

We go from booth to booth, losing epically at just about everything. We finally reach the rides just as Van is reaching that hopped-up excitement where he gets tunnel-visioned and way more determined than any three-year-old has the right to be. To the point where he wants to go on the train ride, and we say he can go on the train ride, but he keeps asking for the train ride.

My frustration prods at me.

"Yes. Van. Train."

"Train, Daddy, train, Daddy, train, Daddy."

"We're going there now," Davey tells him. "You need to wait a minute."

"Train! Me go on train! Traaaaain!" His voice turns shrill as he kicks his little legs, and Davey has to set him on the ground.

"Hey, no kicking." My voice has slipped up a notch.

"Traaaain!"

"Yes. We are going to the train."

"But I don't want to go on the train," Kiera says, stomping her foot.

"We'll go on the train first, and then you get to pick something," I point out.

"Traaaain, Daddy! Van go on train!"

"I hate the train!"

The argument goes on, funneling into this one constant stream of noise in my brain. The incoming explosion is going to be a big one because *dear fucking god, children,* listen when I speak.

But before I can get a word out, Davey tosses Van over his shoulder.

"And home we go."

He walks calmly in the direction of the exit, and Kiera's mouth drops.

"But you promised us rides!"

Davey glances back at her as Van keeps flailing and screaming. "Well, you said you didn't want to go on the train, even though Dad said your ride would come after, so that makes me think you didn't want to go on a ride at all."

"I do, I just don't want to go on a train."

"Then don't go on a train. Wait while Van does, and then it's your turn."

"But I don't want to wait."

"Then we go home."

"That's not fair."

A stray elbow hits the back of Davey's head, but even that doesn't bring the anger out in him. "I know it feels that way. But since Van is little and doesn't understand, he goes first. You're bigger and can understand more, so you go second. Dad and I are biggest and understand how to be patient the most, so we go third. Taking turns is important. Otherwise, we go home."

I watch as she struggles to process it all before she turns determined and nods. "Fine. I'll go on the stupid train."

"Excellent." Davey turns, grabs my hand, and the three of us cross to the stupid fucking train ride as fast as we can. Davey sets Van on his feet when we're right beside it. "There. Train."

The sobbing immediately stops, and the ringing in my ears dies down a notch. It's not until they're both safely strapped in the little carriage, ready to go around the tracks, that we step back from the safety fence and Davey's arm settles around my shoulders.

"You okay?"

"Sorry."

"What for?"

"I sort of … shut down. Left you to deal with it all."

He squeezes me tighter. "Nah, that's not something to be sorry for. We all have our limits, and you hit yours. I didn't."

The ride starts, and suddenly, Kiera and Van are angels, waving and laughing every time they pass us.

"Are we spoiling them too much?"

Davey looks indulgently on. "They're kids. They're still learning. We have our rules and boundaries, and we stick to those, but it's okay to leave our rules at the door on nights like tonight."

"But Van … he had a tantrum over nothing, and now we're rewarding him."

"Was that a tantrum?"

I shoot Davey a confused look. "He was kicking and screaming and elbowing you in the head. Yes. It was a tantrum."

He ducks his chin into his coat to hide his laugh. "I just mean this kind of place isn't a normal environment for a kid. It's a lot. His emotions are a lot. I'm not going to expect him to behave like an adult because he isn't one. Kids are held to an impossible standard, and they're never given a chance to learn."

I wind my arm around his back. Half because I love having him here and half because I'm shamelessly stealing his body heat. "When did you get so smart?"

"You have Beau's word porn; I read parenting books while I'm away."

"You do?"

He frowns a little. "Of course. I don't get the same experience time as you do, so I have to keep up somehow."

"You put me to shame."

"You're a thousand times the father I'll ever be, and we're not arguing about that." He presses a hard, quick kiss to my lips. Here. In public. With who knows from town in plain view, and it makes my heart fucking swim. "No arguing."

My cheeks heat as he pulls away, and I give him what he wants. No arguing.

After the first crisis, we go from ride to ride, and I don't hit explosion level again. I wander slightly ahead as Davey waits for them at the bouncy house until I reach the Ferris wheel. We haven't been on it since before kids, but every Winter Fair when we were together, we'd ride it and kiss at the very top.

Has tonight been perfect? Far from it.

Am I going to wallow in that? Fuck no.

So here's one more ditch attempt to make a moment happen. I make a call, buy two tickets, and then wait. Keller and Will find me before Davey catches up.

"I'm so glad you were here," I say.

"It's Will's first Winter Fair."

"This is awesome," Will says, face lit up with excitement. "Makes me wish Mols and I came before now."

"Eh." Keller shrugs. "He was trying so hard to be grown-up for a while there that I'm not surprised he avoided the place." He turns to me. "Where are the kids?"

"They'll be here in a second. Are you sure you don't mind waiting with them?"

"No way. You know I love kids."

That poor man has forgotten so much. "Give them five minutes and you'll regret that."

"Is that Davey down by the bouncy house?"

"Yup."

"We'll send him up." Keller takes Will's hand, and as they walk away, I hear Will ask, "Think we'll be allowed on the bouncy house too?"

Keller's going to have his hands full with his boyfriend, but he's happy, so that's all that matters.

Davey walks up a moment later, gaze sliding from me up to the Ferris wheel and back again. "Keller and a stranger have kidnapped our children."

"You know Will."

"Barely."

I grin because he's trying to act suspicious, but he keeps glancing over my head.

I hold up the tickets. "Want to take a ride with me?"

He snorts, and it takes me a second to realize how that sounded.

"I mean on the Ferris wheel! That sounded a whole lot more romantic in my head."

"I'm not so sure it did. Either way, taking a ride with you sounds top of my list."

Idiot. I squash my amusement, and we hand over our tickets as an empty basket reaches the bottom. Davey climbs in behind me, sitting so close our thighs are touching.

It's not until the ride starts again that he says anything.

"Remember … remember how we always used to do this?"

"Yup." I lean in closer for more of that body warmth. "I wanted that again."

"Remember how it started?"

Surprisingly, I hadn't until he asked that question. "Wait … you're scared of heights, aren't you?"

He chuckles, little puffs of white coming from between his lips. "Very."

"Shit. We can get off?"

Davey quickly shakes his head and looks at me. His brown eyes look bright in the multicolored lights flashing around us, and he's so close I can make out every freckle. The ground falls behind, and he doesn't look away.

"Remember how you distracted me? That first time?"

My gut squirms pleasantly. "A kiss at the top."

"Yeah …" The word is a whisper. A question. A sound that makes my heart sing. We kiss a lot now. More than we did in those last few years of being married, but still nowhere near as much as I'd like.

This feels different.

Like a meeting of who we were and who we are and who we're going to be. And who I'm going to be is a better husband and father. Because I'll be a better person to myself as well. And as we sit there, watching each other, slowly climbing toward the top, I know I want to remarry him. I know I want to spend the rest of my life with him. I know I want to give him everything he wants and everything that never occurred to him to ask for.

After waiting what feels like forever, we come to a shuddering stop, high above the fair. Davey's hands are fists in his lap, and I slide a hand over one of them, wriggling my fingers until they're linked with his.

When my lips find his, it's warm. Welcoming. The type of kiss that sends shivers from my mouth down to my toes. He's a blazing heat against my eternal chill, and as the kiss deepens, as his hand finds the back of my head, and we lean closer, press deeper, a tear slips out onto my cheek.

Nothing about these past few months has been perfect. Nothing about tonight has been perfect either.

But this moment … it's perfect for *us*.

And maybe that's what I should have been focused on this entire time.

29

Davey

It's Christmas Eve, and Mack is in and out all day. Sometimes he takes the kids, sometimes he leaves them, but there's a general feeling of energy in the air, a happiness radiating from him that I haven't seen in a really, really long time.

He's excited.

And true to my word, I'm not asking questions.

Kiera, Van, and I make a gingerbread house, destroying the kitchen in the process. Then we try to wrap presents for Grandma and Pa, but Van is determined to help, and Kiera is getting frustrated that he keeps doing it wrong.

Mack arrives home in time to save me, swooping in to drop off lunch from Killer Brew, then scooping the kids up and leaving again.

The quiet of the house gets to me.

Reminds me of too many empty hotel rooms.

I fix myself a coffee, then fill the stillness by whipping up some eggnog. I'm not the biggest fan of the drink, but Mack loves it, and when I was younger, Gran would make sure she saved some virgin eggnog for the kids before plowing the rest with rum.

I love the throwbacks this holiday has. Love the traditions and all my memories with family. I wonder if, when, Kiera and Van are older, they'll remember the lights and the snow and the smell of cinnamon and gingerbread and think of me.

You know, if this fucking place ever decides to snow on Christmas again.

Once that's ready, I finish wrapping the few presents I haven't done yet. Mack's are peeking out from the back of the tree, and while it was tempting to buy him a Kindle, he has access to just about any book he likes at work.

Instead, I asked Beau to sign a copy of his series since Mack flew through the first one and is halfway through the second, and then I bought him a bookshelf and a reading light that clips onto the pages. Other than a few old books, Mack doesn't have many, and if he gets back into reading like he used to, I might be able to buy him special ones for his collection every year.

It's nothing extravagant, but Mack's never been a guy to want fancy things. I wish I was presenting him with my resignation letter for Christmas, but hell, maybe that could be a birthday gift instead.

I turn on the little train under the tree and let the robotic *choo choos* fill the room.

Getting to sit with my feelings isn't a fun idea because the stiller I become, the more I miss Gran. Miss being swamped in her hugs. Miss her Christmas Eve pudding. Miss the way she always smelled like lemon.

I didn't see her as much as I'd have liked before she died. I was always away. Or busy. Or too emotionally drained by how bad things were at home.

If I wasn't already certain about my decision, the reminder that things can change so suddenly would have gotten me there.

The door unlocks, and I glance up, expecting Kiera and Van to come tearing into the room, but their usual chaos is missing.

Mack appears in the doorway instead, happy expression faltering as he finds me sitting on the floor. "Hey … you okay?"

"Very."

He takes a step forward. "So why are you …" He waves a hand over where I was watching the train.

"Just thinking."

"Great, now stop that."

"What?"

Mack tugs me to my feet and pulls me into a hug. I'm not ready for the fast kiss he leaves on my lips, but before I can react, he's backing me toward the door.

"Well, hello …"

He laughs. "Hello *and* goodbye."

"Excuse me?"

"I love you, but you need to get out."

"Ah …" Part of me wonders if he's had enough and wants me out of the house for good, but as we reach the front door and he lets go of me to shove my coat in my arms, there's a spark in his eyes that I've missed. "What's going o—"

He lets out a warning sound and mimes zipping his lips. "No questions, remember?"

Okay, so definitely not kicking me out, then. "Can I ask where I'm going?"

"Yup. Your first clue is sitting in the car parked on the curb."

I open the door to find Orson and Ford. They give me creepily matching waves. "I don't get it."

"You need to find the kids. It should take you a good hour or so. Get to it."

"You've lost our kids?"

"Hidden. I've *hidden* our kids. Damn, what kind of dad do you think I am?"

"I'm not taking that bait." I glance at Ford and Orson again. "Am I going with them?"

"Nope. They're your clue."

"Clue? Right. Ah … Ford's Garage …?"

"Bingo!" Mack slaps my ass. "Now get moving before, umm, *the person* they're with hops them up on too much sugar."

"They're with Art, aren't they?"

"Goddamn it, just play the game."

I have no fucking clue what he's up to, but this is fun and different and exactly the Mack I fell in love with. Ford and Orson give me another matching wave as I climb into my car, their grins like something out of a horror show. If I hadn't known them for years, I'd be concerned they were about to murder my husband, but Ford loves a good plot, and I guess that's what they've rustled up here.

My first stop is at Ford's Garage, where Taylor has a clue waiting for me.

"You're in on it too?" I ask.

They shrug and pass over a magnolia. "It's kind of romantic, isn't it?"

"Searching for my kids on Christmas Eve? We have very different ideas of what that word means."

They roll their glossy lips in, holding back a smile and obviously in the know for whatever is going on.

"Maybe just a hint?"

Taylor shakes their head. "No chance. Get on with it."

"A magnolia? The florist, maybe?"

They point toward the front windows, and I turn to look in that direction. What the hell is …

"Magnolia Ridge?"

Taylor's smile breaks free. "Good luck!"

What the ever-loving hell is Mack up to?

Griff and Heath meet me in their front office, and the clue sends me to where Griff and I had our first date. Killer Brew, of course, and where I'm expecting to find Art and the kids, my mom and dad are waiting.

"There goes my hopes of Kiera and Van being with you two."

"They're well looked after," Mom says, wearing that same weird expression everyone else has been today. She pulls me in for a quick hug. "I love you very much."

I frown, because, duh. "Are you dying?"

"Of course not, you little shit. I just don't say it enough."

"Okay. Well, I love you both as well. Obviously."

"We know," Dad says, handing over their clue.

This one takes me to Barney and Leif's souvenir shop near Kil Pen, and then theirs takes me to Killer Adventures.

I thank Beau again, wishing this scavenger hunt was over already, and as I walk to my car, I swear I catch a glimpse of Art's. I try not to be too obvious about looking, but I'm pretty sure Van and Kiera are in the back, and now I think back to it,

I'm sure Art's car had been in the parking lot at Killer Brew as well.

Are they … following me? While I look for them?

I hold my laugh in as I climb into my car, determined to play this game out to the end. I promised I wouldn't ask questions, but every location has me more and more curious. And as I drive all over town, encountering our friends and family at every stop, it makes me fall even more in love with Kilborough than ever.

Keller is waiting at the rotunda by the boardwalk, in the same place where I proposed to Mack all those years ago. His wavy, black hair is pulled back, stubble thicker than usual but trimmed neatly, and he's wearing a long black coat. The man always manages to look like some kind of Norse god without trying.

"I'm freezing my balls off" are the first words out of his mouth.

I pull him into a hug anyway. "Thank you though. I still don't know what's going on, but I'm curious as hell."

"What's going on is … well, Mack's putting things right again."

"I proposed to him here, you know."

"I know. He said."

"Kinda wish I could go back there, do things differently."

"Why?"

"Because maybe then we never would have ended up divorced."

Keller hands over a note. "Yeah, but … I think you needed it."

"Excuse me?"

"Maybe not the divorce, exactly, but the break. The time. I was talking to Mack, and it's been good for him."

I huff. "Well, that's what I want to hear. That my husband is better off without me."

"Did I say that?" He claps my shoulder. "From where I'm standing, the divorce was less of an ending and more of a … reset."

"Really?"

"I think you'll both be a lot happier for it. Whatever comes."

"No."

Keller lifts his eyebrows and doesn't say anything.

"Not whatever comes. We're meant to be together."

"Okay."

"I don't care if you don't believe me."

Keller laughs. "You keep putting words into my mouth. I know you belong together. We all do. We were just waiting for you two to catch up." He jogs down the few stairs and heads toward his car. "Now, excuse me, I have a certain leggy blond waiting to warm my balls back up."

Well, that was more information than I needed, and I'm low-key worried that I'm not going to understand the clue, but I guess it's too late to call him back now.

Only when I open it, there's my handwriting staring back at me.

Bilbo didn't give up. And neither will I.

The words hold so much more meaning being reflected back at me. And this clue is simple.

The library.

It's not supposed to be open today, so I'm apprehensive as I approach, but there's Tonya waiting at the door.

"Tell me you know which book it is?" she says.

"I have a good idea."

She unlocks the front door, and I make my way to the aisle

I've become overly familiar with. *The Hobbit* is right where it always is, and I pull out the book, flip open the cover, and there's my next clue.

Bilbo traveled far, but he always found his way back home again. And so do you.

Home.

I swallow, taking the note and setting the book back before I thank Tonya and return to the car.

I'm not in a rush this time, knowing that was the final clue.

I pass Art's car on the way down my street, and he throws me a peace sign that I don't know what to make of.

Once I'm in the driveway, with the car turned off, I sit for a moment wondering how, even though I've been alone for half the day, this might turn out to be my favorite Christmas Eve yet.

Mack needed me out of the house.

But he didn't want to leave me completely alone.

I guess in Kilborough, we never are.

The minute I push our front door open, a burst of scents hit my nose. The type of familiar smell that takes me back in a rush and makes it impossible to keep moving. I freeze in the hall, trying to place it, but not sure if I'm right.

Gran. Her cooking. Her smell. Her Christmas.

Am I hallucinating?

I inhale again, sure this must be some kind of nostalgic mind-fuck, but the scent is still there.

And before I can take another step, I'm rushed from three sides. Kiera launches into my arms, Van clings to my leg, and Mack grabs me from behind. I'm squeezed half to death as we stumble around the corner into the living room, where all the lights are on, the music is playing, and the little train is still *choo chooing* around the tree.

"Merry Christmas, Davey," Mack whispers.

The first thing I see is my Millennium Falcon, completely rebuilt and sitting pride of place on the coffee table.

The second is a pudding that looks suspiciously like Gran's right beside it.

The third is a speck of snow, drifting past the window.

Then it's Kiera's and Van's smiling faces as she innocently asks, "Did you have fun, Daddy? We were racing you."

I don't see anything after that because I burst into fucking tears.

30

Mack

Davey doesn't say anything about the pudding tasting like shit, and he's speechless that his Falcon is rebuilt. We cave and give the kids a present each early, then curl up on the couch together with his spiked eggnog while a Christmas movie plays.

My heart is so fucking full while I hold him, and then once the kids are in bed, I take his hand and lead him into our room.

"You're incredible," he rasps, pulling back until I hit his chest. He wraps his arms around me, nose sliding down the side of my neck.

"Was that okay? Sorry I had you drive all over town, but I needed you out of the house, and I didn't like the idea of you being on your own for hours at Christmas."

"It was perfect. I'd worry about you being an evil mastermind if you weren't so damn precious."

"Precious." My laugh rumbles softly through my chest. "You've always seen too much good in me."

"Or exactly the right amount. Here …" Davey holds his phone up in front of us.

"What are you doing?"

"I want a photo with you. To remind me of tonight."

"Oh. Ahh …"

He kisses my neck this time, and a pleasant shiver runs through me.

"Photo, yes. Okay."

Davey cuddles me tight from behind as he lifts his phone and takes a couple of shots. Then, like it's been planned, I turn my head to kiss his cheek, and he goes to do the same. Our lips meet, and I have no idea if he gets a shot of that or not because as soon as we connect, the photos completely leave my mind.

There's nothing I don't love about kissing Davey. His soft lips, his strong tongue, the taste of eggnog and rum between us. But the thing I love most is how familiar he is. I don't need excitement—though I'm thrumming with that too—I just need the way my chest is full when I'm with him.

Having sex wasn't part of my plan for the day, but I feel so close to him it just seems right.

Unlike the frenzy of last time, I'm not in a hurry to get him naked. I let myself enjoy it for what it is, my hands exploring every strip of exposed skin they find, and Davey does the same.

Kissing, touching, loving. I moan at the sound of his pants hitting the floor before he breaks away from me and pushes his underwear down too. He's got dark chest hair and thick thighs, a once-six-pack that's softly padded but makes a reappearance when he clenches. Like when I run my fingers down his soft V and his whole body draws tight. His cock pulses at the movement.

I'm breathing heavily already when he unbuttons my pants. Davey sinks to his knees, my pants following in a torturously slow path after him.

When my dick springs back and hits my stomach, it's an effort not to beg him to suck it. Not to tilt my hips closer to him.

His beautiful eyes study it for a moment before drifting closed as he leans forward and sucks it into his mouth.

The heat he surrounds me with has lust pooling in my balls, and even though he takes his time, stroking me reverently with his tongue and kissing my tip before ducking down to suck on my balls, my toes curl over into the carpet. I could easily blow from this. From all that buildup and need over the years being fulfilled, piece by piece, every time we're together.

His wet finger slips into my crease, and I relax against the feel of him stroking it over my hole.

"Gonna make love to you tonight," he murmurs. "Going to fill up this sexy hole."

My thighs twitch. "Fuck yes."

He presses his finger in, following that same path he has countless times before, and it kills me all the years we spent not doing this. All the times we had to enjoy each other and chose not to. Things had turned stale, but without us knowing that, without us both wanting to move on, nothing ever would have changed.

Now I know better.

Davey goes back to worshiping my cock while he stretches me open, his own hanging heavy between his legs. I want to touch it, want to taste him, but he's taken the control tonight, and I'm more than happy to take his lead. So instead of giving in to the urge to stroke him, I card my fingers through his hair instead.

"God, I love your curls."

His eyes spark with amusement as he looks up at me, lips stretched wide around my girth. The eyes, the curls, the freckles, all as beautiful as the first day I saw him like this. The lines across his forehead and beside his eyes might be deeper, but that only makes me love this sight more.

To know there are so many years between that first time and now, yet my heart aches for him like it's never done before.

Davey slowly pulls off my dick. "I want you on your back."

His fingers leave my ass, signaling that it's almost time for more, and a thrill passes over me as I flop back onto the bed. Davey grabs the lube, not bothering to ask about a condom this time. He trusts that I've kept my word like I've trusted him to keep his.

He crawls up between my legs on his knees, then pushes my thighs apart and back.

"Missed this hole," he says, opening the lube and squeezing it over his cock. He stares between my legs as he strokes himself, and my cock throbs at the sight.

I grab my knees and spread my legs further, rewarded by the long groan Davey makes right before he bites his knuckles.

I watch as he grips himself and leans forward, the smooth tip of his cock pressing flush with my hole. My body immediately goes pliant, needing to feel him inside me, and Davey doesn't falter. Like he feels the same weight I do, he presses in. He doesn't stop, even though the stretch is a lot, but he's slow enough that it doesn't turn painful.

Rightness surrounds me as his pubes brush my ass, and he buries himself as deep as he can go.

"The way you take my cock is indescribable," he says, leaning forward onto one forearm while his hand finds the pulse in my throat. "Love to feel the way your heart's racing."

"Because you make me forget to breathe."

He rocks slowly inside me, a gentle tilt of his hips as his eyes meet mine. The emotion I see staring down at me is something that was missing in our relationship toward the end, and the relief at having it back is overwhelming.

My hands dive into his hair again, and I tug him down to kiss me. It's so intimate, so raw, I get lost in the kiss, dick still hard as a rock but ignored as it rests against my hip. Davey's lazy thrusts don't pick up either; we're not fucking to get off. Just to connect. And I've never felt as connected to him before as I do at this moment.

We switch positions before long so that I'm on top, looking down on him as I work myself up and down on his cock. Then, he takes me from behind, sucking a bruise into my neck and whispering, over and over, how much he loves me.

There's nothing between us. No condom, no secrets, no distrust or resentment, and I let myself enjoy what we've been missing for so long.

"Turn over," he rumbles, pulling out, and I hurry to do as he says.

I'm heady off the smell of his sweat, and when he pushes back inside, his arms on either side straining under his weight, his scent surrounds me. I breathe deep, and the ache in my cock turns desperate.

"I need to come," I beg.

He nods. "Whatever you want, baby."

Davey's next thrust is harder, more determined, sending me

further up the bed. His pace picks up as this quiet love burns away and the need for relief takes over.

My heart feels too big, my dick too hard, and I jerk myself through the high he's giving me. No random hookup could ever have come close to the way I feel when I'm with him.

His thrusts get harder, faster, pounding out a frenzied rhythm against my ass, and the *slap slap slap*, along with his hoarse breathing, is taking over my senses.

"Come on," he gasps out.

I strangle my cock, beating off as hard and fast as I can. My head falls back deep into the pillow as the pressure gets too much. A wave of heat rolls over me, and my balls pulse, letting out the first bit of relief onto my skin.

Davey grunts as I coax myself through my orgasm, jaw clamped tight, sweat building at his hairline as he tries to get himself there. My ass is sensitive, my dick limp, but I love the feel of him owning me anyway.

"Don't want … to end …" he grunts.

So I reach down, slip my hand between us, and run my fingertips over his tight balls. "Love being fucked by you," I tell him. "Love having you inside me. You're the only one, Davey. Your hole. Always. Fill me with your cum."

"*Nrg*, fuck." He grunts, then slams home, hips pressed tight against me as he empties his load into my ass.

I sigh at how amazingly claimed I feel, and when Davey's done, he drops down on top of me.

"I never wanted that to end," he says.

"I got that impression, yeah."

He huffs a laugh as his cock slips out, and then he rolls me onto my front. "On your knees. I want to see it run out."

Where this would have made me self-conscious at one point, there's none of that now. I cross my arms over my pillow and prop up onto my knees, and then I push his cum back out again. The feel of it running down my thighs gives me shivers, especially when he runs his fingers through it.

"I love you so much," he whispers.

"You better be talking to me and not my ass."

Davey laughs and leaves to get a washcloth. "Tell me we can do that again tomorrow," he says, running the hot washcloth up my thighs.

"Anytime you want."

It's not until he's cleaned me up and we've changed the sheets and gotten dressed that I let reality rush back in.

Anytime he wants. For a week. Just a week.

And then he has to leave again.

I pretend I'm asleep so neither of us has to talk about it.

31

Davey

I NEED TO HAVE A WORD WITH WHOEVER TURNED UP TIME. Christmas disappeared before I could blink, and then New Year's passed in the pop of a firework, and now … Mack pulls up out the front of the hire car place in Springfield, neither of us having said much on the drive.

"Where are we, Daddy?" Kiera asks, and it squeezes my heart.

I plaster on a smile before turning to her. "I have to pick up a car. I'm going back to work today, remember?"

"But I don't want you to go."

"I know. Neither do I."

"Then why are you?"

That's the question, isn't it? Mack is stiff beside me, staring blankly out the front window, and every part of this feels wrong. And exactly the same as it always does. I just need to make it out of the car.

"I'm going to make some money, and then I'll be back soon."

Her little face crumples. "I don't like when you go away."

Fuck.

I get out of the car and round to her door so I can swamp her in a hug. "You'll be back at school soon. You'll hardly notice I'm gone."

"Daddy work?" Van asks.

"Yeah, buddy. I have to go to work today."

"No, Daddy. No work."

"I have to."

He tugs on the straps of his seat. "Me go too. Van go with Daddy. Van go to work."

My throat is too clogged up to respond, so I lean over, plant a kiss on his forehead, then close the door on their crying.

Do I feel like the worst dad in the fucking world? You betcha I do.

Mack climbs out, and his eyes are as glassy as mine, but at least he can manage a smile.

"They'll be okay," he says.

"Yeah, but will I?" Going to bed with him every night for the last week, getting lost in each other's bodies, our affection through the day slowly slotting back to what it was … how am I supposed to go from all that to nothing?

"You will." He tugs me into a hug. "Because you're amazing, and you always put us first."

I snort, and he squeezes me harder.

"It will be better this time," he promises.

I almost tell him, right then, that it really will be, because this isn't going to last long. The whole time I'm gone, I'll be searching for any and all leads that have me back home with them.

But I don't know how long that will take, so I hold off from saying anything. With the lump in my throat, I doubt I'd be able to get the words out anyway.

I just return the force of his hug, like we're both trying to meld together.

"They're going to keep you so busy on this new account for the next two weeks that you'll hardly notice you're gone. Then you'll be back home again. It'll be fine."

I still can't answer. Just duck down, pull up the handle on my suitcase, and then, before I can step away, I cup the back of his neck and draw him into one last kiss.

Mack is right. It's two weeks. And sure, it's always been hard before but never *this* hard. Like I'm tearing myself in half.

I blame the long time off. I've become too used to having them there at every point of my day. That's all this is.

I can't look back at the car as I let him go and head for the rental office.

Eric told me the New York office would be operating on a skeleton staff for the next week. Him, me, and two members of my team hustling to get this massive account up and running. Then next week, I'll brief the others on what we've decided for the campaign, make sure it's assigned and delegated down to the last detail, and then I'll be ready to head home again. Mack's right. It will go quickly. The office always breathes life back into me, but while usually I'm excited to brainstorm with like-minded people, the thrill of a new campaign is dulled by the memory of what actually happens when I'm back home again.

All the late calls.

The constant emails.

The laptop perched on my lap after dinner while I'm supposed to be spending time with the family. During the entire drive, my grip on the steering wheel keeps getting tighter until, when I reach New York, my fingers are cramped, and my knuckles are aching.

Sleeping in an empty, impersonal hotel bed is depressing. Waking up alone, with no Mack and no tiny Van plastered to me, hollows out my chest in a way that's never happened before.

I'm sluggish as I shower and get dressed in my suit. As I stop by the usual hole-in-the-wall cafe for my morning coffee. As I swipe into the enormous steel-and-glass building where our office is located.

Normally, being back here puts a spring in my step. Reminds me that I'm part of something bigger than me.

I'm just not feeling it.

My swanky new office doesn't do a damn thing either. And I'm sitting at my desk, waiting for my computer to reload after the long time off, when Eric taps on my open door.

"Davey, welcome back."

I nod in his direction, then turn back to my screen.

His hesitation bleeds into the room. "Did you get your Christmas bonus?"

"I did. Thank you." I only add the last part so I don't sound ungrateful. It was a lot of money, and I won't pretend like it didn't help pad our savings, but it was also a lot of money I earned. With me continually putting my life on hold for this job, the least they can do is compensate me for it.

Eric walks in and takes the chair opposite mine. "We'll

always take care of you," he says. "You're a valued member of this company. Irreplaceable."

There's no way he can hear the ringing in my ears, but even without pointing out how truly bone-deep-pissed-off I am, he knows. Normally, I wouldn't dream of saying anything. Normally, I bite my tongue and put the job first. Tell him the family is great, and I'm doing okay.

But I'm really, really not okay.

I've worked my ass off for my entire adult life, and for what? A divorce and heartbroken kids? Even the full bank account can't fix my guilt over constantly leaving them in that position. And if I feel like this, how frustrated must Mack be, having to console our children by himself over something outside of his control?

I fucking get it.

The anger and resentment that he felt is building in me too. Not for him. For Eric. For this company that supposedly takes care of me.

Eric sighs. "I know you're disappointed. I get it. I wouldn't have asked if I wasn't backed into a corner."

My computer finishes doing its thing, so I open my emails, preparing to deal with a tsunami hitting my inbox.

"Davey … come on, now."

I give him my full attention. "Come on, *what*?"

"You're going to give me the silent treatment?"

"You're discussing a topic I want no part in. I'm here. I'm prepared to work. Now, unless our conversation has to do with this new account, I can only assume we're wasting company resources and my own damn time."

He spreads his hands. "What would you have had me do?"

"Personally? Tell the client that our office reopens on the ninth. Move forward on the account with the staff that we have available at the time. And let me have my remaining six damn weeks with my own damn family that I have goddamn earned after leaving them, constantly, for the last ten years."

His face falls. "It doesn't work like that."

"Clearly." I eye him. "You've been a good boss. I understand the position you were in, and I also know that if I continue to advance here, I will be sitting where you are one day. I'll have to face the same decision you did." Certainty wraps around me. "And that just isn't something I'm interested in dealing with."

"What are you saying?"

Nerves are pumping through my veins, and I have to grip the side of my desk to stop my hands from shaking. "This is my two weeks' notice." My hushed words come as a surprise, even to me. For one wild moment, logistics don't matter. Finances don't matter. They will, the second I walk away from here and realize that I've fucked my whole family over, but Mack's right. I've put them first. I've put myself through hell to make sure I provided for them. I've given them everything I thought they needed.

But they don't want my money.

They want me.

So what the fuck am I still putting myself through this stress for?

"I know you're upset, but don't do something you'll regret," Eric says.

"I've already done too many things I regret. Trust me when I say this won't even make my top five."

"Davey." He's lost for words. "Is it money? Do you need more? A promotion—"

"My family."

"What?"

"I need my family."

He's visibly sweating. "And what about what they need? You've got your health insurance and their college to think about. Who's going to pay your mortgage?"

All those questions twist my gut. "I don't know," I answer honestly, trying not to get choked up. "But I've reached my limits. I'm stuck. I can't keep going like this."

"I can get you a bigger bonus this quarter. We've got some large accounts signing in the next few weeks. I'll give them to you."

I actually laugh. "That's the complete opposite of what I want. More work?" I huff, taking note of the nine-hundred-and-something emails I have to sort through. It's all too much. "It's clear from this conversation you're either not listening or don't want to hear it." I rub my eyes, fighting through the weariness. "I will make sure this client is happy. I will design one of the best PR briefs you've ever seen. It will launch internationally, and they will sell a fuck ton more product than they ever planned for. But then I'm done."

"Davey—"

"No. Done. You've done a lot for me, Eric, and I appreciate it. I've loved working here. The pay and benefits are outstanding, I have a fantastic team, and I genuinely love working with them." I shrug. "Some of the clients I could give or take, but it doesn't matter how much I love those things, I love Mack and the kids more. I want my family back. I want my husband back. Jobs can be replaced. He can't."

Eric tries to say something, but I hold up my hand.

"I've made my decision. Please don't make me lose the respect I have for you. Understand that I've thought about this. A lot. It's not spur-of-the-moment." Even though it definitely is. "And I really do thank you for everything you've done."

"That's it, then?"

I guess it is.

Eric stands and holds his hand out to me. "You're a hell of a man, Davey. One of the best marketing minds I've met."

"Thank you."

"I don't want to see it go to waste."

"If it does or it doesn't, that's my choice."

He leaves, and I turn back to my work, expecting to feel a hell of a lot lighter.

And I do. For approximately the time it takes to draft and send my resignation letter, then the *oh fucks* kick in.

In two weeks, I'll be unemployed. I've *never* been unemployed in my entire life.

I ignore the way my gut churns and get back to work, constantly reminding myself that once these two weeks are up, I'm heading home.

For good.

32

Mack

Everything hurts and I'm mopey, but I'm still somehow hopeful for the future. With Davey gone, I spend extra time making sure to smother Kiera and Van in love. I read, a lot, and fill my days with lunch dates and looking up cooking recipes.

I'm no master chef, and I pretty much hate getting home from work and having to think of what to make, but I love feeding my family, and the smile on Davey's face when he ate a terrible version of his gran's pudding was worth all the headaches to make it.

So I want to try putting real effort into it. Maybe I'll still hate it, but maybe, if I plan ahead, I can view it as less of a task and more another piece of what makes me *me*.

Davey and I also text all day and talk for hours at night. As soon as he's back in his hotel room and the kids are tucked away in bed, we shamelessly get ourselves off on a video call. I'm not sure if the extra attention is making things better or worse.

I miss him so deeply that even though I'm working on myself, even though I'm focusing on things I love, none of those things are hitting close to the comfort I need from them.

"Holy shit, did you hear?" Tonya shrieks, jumping out at me and all but hurricaning the things on my desk. "Rhonda's retiring!"

I blink. Shake my head. Blink again. "But she's only fifty-nine."

Tonya throws up both hands. "Apparently, some relative died and left her a wad of cash, so she's packing it up and moving somewhere hot."

"Somewhere hot is the dream."

"Someone dying and leaving me money is mine."

Well, that's morbid. I shoot her a look, idea starting to take hold. "Do … do you know … will they advertise for Rhonda's position, do you think?"

"I assume so. They should just give it to you though."

"Me?" My cheeks flush. "What about you?"

"Well, I don't want it. Even if I did, I don't do half of the things around here that you do. What was the newest idea you started this month?"

"Coffee and cakes?"

Tonya rolls her eyes. "Who else would have gotten Art de Almeida to agree to *delivering* a coffee and cakes order for the group meetings we have here. We have *three* orders today."

Is it stupid that something so simple makes me excited? The cleanup will take longer, but knowing that people genuinely like my idea gives me a boost of pride.

"You really don't want the manager position?"

Tonya hurries to shake her head. "I like the limited hours and lack of responsibility, thanks." She looks like she wants to say more.

"What is it?"

"Well … how would Davey feel if you were working full-time?"

"He'd support me." I'm sure about that because he doesn't know how to be any other way. "It'd mean putting Van into care a few more days a week, and I'm … I'm torn on that."

"Well, we've had to wait for Rhonda's dead aunt/uncle/whoever to drop dead for this position to come available. I don't think you can count on that happening again."

"I know …"

She leaves, and I'm left to stew in my thoughts. The whole point in Davey working the way he does is so that I don't have to overdo it and can make sure our kids are raised by us and not someone else. We're so fucking lucky that we have that option. But this position … I want it. I'd be amazing at it. It would mean working five full days a week though, which not only takes me away from Van through the day, and both of them some afternoons, but it also means no more one-on-one time with Davey when he's home.

Am I understanding how conflicted he could be over work and family? I sure fucking am. I groan and press my fingers into my eyes. If only this job paid better and I could take over for Davey for a while, but even full-time, it wouldn't stretch to all of our expenses.

Sure enough, that afternoon, Rhonda's resignation announcement comes through. I'm thrilled for her, but she doesn't say much about how the position will be filled or who will take over for her or anything. What if my new boss ends up being a total dick?

Rhonda always left us alone for the most part. She, Tonya, and I are like a little family, and sure, there are two other people who work here on the weekends, but I rarely see them. It's always the three of us.

My need to cling to anything familiar and resist change is coming in strong.

I force it away.

That night, after jerking off and telling Davey I love him, we're both lying there, me in cold pajamas, on either side of our phones, a peaceful silence settling around us when I say, "Rhonda quit today."

"Rhonda … your boss?"

I nod, not looking at the screen. "Yeah … Tonya thinks I should apply for her spot."

"Do it."

I glance up at his immediate eagerness. "But—"

"Do it."

I huff a laugh. "You're amazing, but there's a lot to think about. To work out. What do we do with Van? And Kiera? When would I even see you during the times you're home? And am I even good enough? I don't have formal training— some people go to college for this stuff, but I was hired off the street."

"That's an exaggeration," he teases. "Look, there are always, *always* reasons not to do something." He pauses to allow for a steadying breath. "But do you want it, Mack?"

"I … I think so."

"Then apply. Maybe you don't get it, but maybe you do. It'll happen the way it's supposed to, and if you get the job, we'll work out the rest."

"You're amazing. You know that?"

Davey chuckles. "You only tell me that every time we

speak." He runs a hand down his face, and the tightness around his eyes makes him look more stressed than ever. "Look, I need to get some sleep, but if you want the job, take it." His voice gets more tense. "When I get home … there's a lot we need to talk about."

"Well, that doesn't sound good."

He bares his teeth. "Not … *not* good. It's a conversation we need to have in person, but it has nothing directly to do with us and where our relationship is."

"I'm not sure that made it sound any better."

A smile tugs at the corners of his lips. "You asked me to trust you, remember? To not ask questions and that you'd tell me when you could."

"This doesn't feel like the same thing though."

"Maybe not, but will you trust me anyway?"

Trust him? When my gut is in knots? When I'm scared that whatever he's going to say is going to tear us apart again, no matter what he said? "Do you still love me?" I whisper.

"More than ever."

The absolute truth in his tone eases my anxiety. "Then yeah. I trust you. Of course."

"I can't wait to be back there with you," he says.

I know what he means. The talking and texting and sex is great, but it only makes me ache to hold him more. It's easy to see why I got to the point of divorce the first time because my need to be with him is already eating at me.

The difference this time is that I won't let it take over.

"I miss you. So much. But I'm here waiting."

"You've always been too good to me."

That comment is so stupid I almost laugh. "No, I haven't. But I'm determined to give you everything you deserve from now on."

He blinks at the screen, and it feels like he's staring right at me and not some stupid camera. "I promise you exactly the same."

We hang up, and I drop my phone to my chest, exactly over the place it hurts. Just one more week.

I only need to make it through one more week until he's home.

33

Davey

"Do you have a minute?"

I glance up from sending one of my last-ever emails for the company. My heart is heavy, my energy is low, but in a few hours, I'll be heading home to my family.

For good.

That makes it easier to go through with this.

"Sure, Eric, come in." Even after my little *I quit* tantrum, he's been a great boss. We announced my resignation, put my job to recruitment, and he's told everyone—high and low—that the company is losing a huge talent. Which, I can't lie, is amazing to hear, even if it also stings that little bit too.

"Everything done?" He points toward my computer, and I stare at it for a moment, realizing that, yeah. I think I am done. I'm officially replaced.

"I think so." I shut down the screen, realizing I don't have a hell of a lot to pack up from here. I didn't have my promotion for long, but even more than that, I didn't make a lot of effort to make any space here *mine*.

"Good. This is for you."

Eric hands over a card, and I'm blown away by all the people who have written inside it. I save reading what they've actually written for later, though, because I refuse to get emotional at work. I set the card down and smile over at him. "I appreciate you not making this harder than it needs to be."

"How did Mack take the news?"

"I, uh … haven't told him yet. It's a conversation we need to have in person."

His eyes widen. "You don't think he'll be pissed off that you quit your amazing job without telling him?"

"Nope."

"How the hell do you know that?"

"Because when Mack says he'll support me through anything, he means it."

"Uh-huh …" Neither of us mentions the divorce, and I'm grateful because that's a time in my life I want squarely behind me. "Well, since you're in the habit of making decisions solo …" Eric opens his jacket and pulls out a wad of paper that he *thumps* on my desk.

Apprehension settles over me. "What is this? A noncompete? You know I have nothing—"

"Just read it."

I flick my gaze to him and back to the paper again. The more I read, the more I'm sure he's confused. "This is my position description."

"Is it?"

I jab at where it says *marketing director*. "Yes."

"I wouldn't be giving you this if I didn't think you were good at reading contracts, Davey. Look closer."

I'm so fucking confused, but I play his game, switching from skimming to actually reading what's in front of me.

... contracting the services of Davey Eiser, marketing director, on all premium client portfolios ...

"Contracting ..." I query the word out loud.

"I meant it when I said you were irreplaceable."

I wave a hand at my computer. "We've just proved that isn't the case."

"Anyone can do a task. Not everyone has the creative vision you do. In short, I don't want to lose that."

"So what are you offering?"

Eric points at the contract. "Take that home. Discuss it with Mack. Make any changes you're comfortable with, and then come back to me. You've brought a lot of big clients in, and you've also highlighted the need for some restructuring." He pins me with a look. "It wasn't fair of me to break our arrangement."

I swallow thickly. "Thank you."

"We want to hire you as a consultant. Top-level expertise that the teams have to run their ideas by before we move on. Ideally, you'll make time to pop into the office, at least once a month, but no more away trips. No more face time with clients. The retainer we're offering you *is* a pay cut, but that comes under the assumption of decreased hours."

My vision goes unfocused on the paper, struggling to wrap my head around what it says. "Why now? Why ... Just why?"

"I'll be honest with you: this wasn't an option before. We have no need for consultancy at an executive level. The director role brought you leverage, and the years you've put in, the testimony from happy client after happy client ... it all adds up." Eric spreads his hands wide. "I understand if you don't take it. But I'm asking you to at least think about it because I couldn't let you walk away without one more ditch attempt to keep you here."

"Wow …" This is so far beyond what I was expecting when he walked in here that I'm struggling to wrap my head around it. "I'll … yeah. I'll talk to Mack." Because if I take this, that'll be it. This'll be our new future, and if it means working from home and being on call, I want guarantees that it's not going to bleed into my family life like it always has before. There's no point getting my hopes up over something that could be another trap.

Eric gets up to leave.

"Hey. Thank you. I'm not sure if I can take it, but I really appreciate this."

He smiles, taps the doorframe, and then leaves.

I stare at the contract again, wanting to dive in and read it but feeling way too overwhelmed at the idea.

My team takes me out for farewell drinks right after, but I stick to one to make sure I can drive home afterward. Mack didn't sound happy when I said I wouldn't be home until late, but once I tell him why, I know he'll understand.

I leave at eight, a twinge of sadness at saying goodbye to everyone that's quickly smothered by how much easier it is to breathe once I've gone.

I hit the road home, and contract or no contract, the relief I've been waiting for finally settles in.

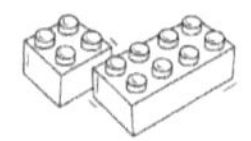

I'M EXPECTING THE HOUSE TO BE DARK AND QUIET WHEN I pull up in the driveway and wheel my suitcase inside. But the TV is on, and when I shed my coat, then step from the hallway into the living room, there's Mack on the couch, eyes sleepy but smile ready.

"You're home!" He tackles me in a hug, mouth finding mine, and we both topple over onto the couch. He doesn't give me a second to get a word in as he kisses his way down my body and gives me the blow job of my life.

After a shitfuck of a day, big thoughts and bigger good-byes, this is the perfect way to end it.

Or … given it's after midnight, the perfect way to start a new one.

I come with my cock buried in his throat, thighs twitching over the high of my orgasm, and when Mack pulls off me, he looks smug as hell.

"My turn."

He shakes his head, cheeks tinging pink. "I might have, uh, taken care of myself already. I got too horny waiting for you."

"Mack!"

"Sorry." He doesn't look it.

And it's not like I can be mad at him after the way he just sucked me dry. I give him a long, sweet kiss, reveling in the fact that this is it now. I can do this anytime I want.

He pulls away and settles beside me while I tuck my dick back into my pants. "You wanted to talk about something."

I should have known that he'd be fixated on it. I meet his eyes and say, "I quit."

Mack blinks. Then blinks again. "You … what?"

"Sorry if I should have told you first. Or talked to you about it. I know it puts us in a difficult place now financially, but—"

"I don't care."

"What?"

"I don't fucking care." Tears spill onto his cheeks. "You quit? You're home? For good?"

I hurry to nod. "Yeah. You're dating an unemployed guy now."

"I don't fucking care as long as it's you. Holy shit. Holy *shit*. Holy fucking *shit*." He's completely sobbing. "You quit."

My heart goes all floaty at how he's laughing through his tears. "I did. And there's going to be a lot we have to work out together."

Mack kisses me, deep and slow and full of all the emotion building in my chest. "We'll figure it out. Just let me enjoy this."

So I do. We spend the night enjoying each other, and when the kids wake up the next morning and I tell them Daddy doesn't have to leave again, I get mixed reactions from two little people who have no clue what's going on. Kiera asks if it means she won't get toys anymore, and Van demands to go to work with me.

Oh, the love …

But I don't need anything more than that from them. All I need is to never have to leave them upset again.

34

Mack

It's weird being the one away for work, and I've gotta say, a night on my own is luxury. I'll never say that to Davey or the kids, but nabbing myself a ticket for this book fair was a smart choice.

I have a big, fluffy bed and room service, after an entire day spent discussing books. I'm in heaven.

Sure, I miss them, but I'm happy to miss them every once in a while to have an entire day off to myself like this.

The past year has been a fucking blur of upheaval. From the second Davey quit his job, everything changed, and I've never been more happy for that in my life. Instead of clinging to what was familiar, I applied for the library supervisor role and got it, which came with a substantial enough pay raise that, combined with his bonus, we could manage Davey taking a few months off to figure out what his next moves were.

I always knew he was going to take Eric's offer. Davey's made to be busy and have his mind working, so one month into the three he'd planned to take off, he drove back to New York, sat down with Eric and HR, and got a plan put into place. He works three days a week, turns off his cell phone at six, and is uncontactable all weekend. In return, he goes to New York once a month and works his three days in the office before coming home again.

He still hates leaving us, and I maybe have some light PTSD from being left all the time, but having him gone for four days is a lot easier than two whole weeks.

It helps that I'm busy too. The days he's gone are full of school drop-off, work, lunch with one of the DMC guys, planning community events, school pickup before the kids hang out at work with me for an hour, home, dinner, bath, and bed. We still miss Davey, but it's not unbearable the way it once was.

I enjoy my night alone in Boston before getting back in the car and driving home. While it's not something I want to do frequently, the occasional night away here and there sounds like a fun plan. Beau's next book tour is coming up, and he asked if I want to travel with him for a couple of days. I'm considering it. Ever since Davey got him to sign books for me, we've gotten close, and it's great to have someone I can totally geek out with. Between the both of us and the handful of other book lovers we've found, we've started a book club that meets once a month. Payne and Davey like to tease us about our "fantasy porn," but Beau said Payne reads it too.

Davey doesn't pick up when I call, so I assume he's taken Kiera and Van out somewhere, but when I get home, the front door is unlocked.

The house is suspiciously quiet though.

Too quiet.

I dump my keys in the hall and go looking for any hints as to where they all are. The living room and kitchen are both clear, but when I'm about to head upstairs, I see something on the floor.

An arrow made out of LEGOs. I follow the direction it's pointing and find another one. And another.

They lead me to the back door, where there's a LEGO sign sticking up out of the grass with "this way" taped to the front in Kiera's writing, accompanied by Van's scribble.

Whatever this is, it looks fun and was definitely not what I was expecting to come home to. The sign is pointing toward Davey's LEGO hut, so I make my way over, slide open the door, and "What the fuck?" trips out of my mouth before I can stop it.

The LEGO is all gone. The whole room has been cleared out, and instead, my books fill the shelves on three walls, an enormous, comfy-looking chair is in the center, and a few bean bags are on the floor by the door. Keira and Van are giggling from behind the chair, and when I step around it to see them, I find Davey there too.

On his knee.

Holding what looks like my wedding band.

"W-what is this?"

I think my heart has stopped beating.

Davey smiles, and it's beautiful. "This is me, finally, officially, putting our lives back together. When I met you, I knew you were it for me, Mack. Things might have been rough, and we might have lost our way for a little bit there, but you're still forever for me. You always will be. So I want to start over. I want to promise myself to you again because this time, I know exactly what I'm promising. This time, I know what forever means. There's no doubt. Nothing holding me back. My priorities are where they should have always been, and I've worked out what's important. I love you. It's as simple as that."

"I love you too." I think the only reason I'm not crying is because I'm in shock. Davey's never once mentioned wanting to get married again. We call each other husbands out of habit, but I'd been happy to go on exactly as we are so long as it meant we were together.

"Will you marry me, Mack? Umm, again?"

"Yeah." I laugh, nodding hard. "I'll marry you again. And again and again. However many times I need to."

"Jesus." Davey hangs his head. "Why don't we stick with once more and call it a day?"

"Deal."

He surges to his feet and kisses me, Kiera squealing loudly from excitement while Van tries to join our hug with no real idea of what's going on.

"I want to be flower girl!" Kiera shouts.

"There's no one else." I scoop her and Van up, and Davey and I crush them between us.

My eyes scan the room around us, feeling warm and at home immediately. "You made me my own library?"

"Your book collection was getting out of control," Davey says.

"But … your LEGO."

He puts the kids down. "The truth is, I got so into it because it was my way to escape the tension in the house. I don't need to do that anymore, and coming out here to build things just takes me back to that place. So I want you to have this space. And I thought … if there's room at the library, I could set up some of my bigger pieces there, and the rest …

maybe one night a week, I could run a building class with kids or something."

"That's a fucking amazing idea."

"Yeah?" The relief that crosses his face is so sweet. "I want to enjoy it again. Maybe it sounds stupid, but—"

"Nope. I think it's amazing. Like you."

He rolls his eyes. "There's that word again."

I pointedly look around the room. "Well, you keep on proving me right."

He looks down and lifts my hand to slip the ring back onto my finger. The ring finger. Right where it belongs. "We're doing this again?"

"For the last time," I assure him.

Davey smiles and buries his face in my neck, and I hold him close, breathing in his scent, bathing in his warmth, the anxiousness of the past few years dissolving into nothing.

"Finally," I sigh.

"What?"

"Everything is finally perfect."

EPILOGUE

Davey

"Not again." Payne rushes to grab the four-year-old redhead off the bar top. She's wearing a Tinkerbell dress, combat boots, Barbie sunglasses, a bike helmet, and a dinosaur tail. I'm not sure what style it is she's channeling, but when she says, "But, Papa, I'm following the stars to Neverland!" I know exactly which parent she takes after.

The one sitting with his nose in a book at a party.

My husband would probably be the same if I let him. And that's husband, officially, as of last year. It feels different the second time around, like I have my eyes open, and it's easy to appreciate the little things. When we fight, we fight properly and actually come to a resolution instead of Mack having his worries build up and me shutting down to it all.

I love this new version of us.

Mom and Dad have the kids downstairs in the bar area of Killer Brew, leaving Davey and me to chat with our friends.

Almost everyone we know is here. Art's Fourth of July celebrations have turned Killer Brew into a headache of red, white, and blue. Families pack the bar around below, and Art invited a few of us upstairs to take a minute away from the mayhem.

I watch as Art pours out fourteen shot glasses while Joey hands them out. No one is talking much, the noise from downstairs more than enough to fill in the comfortable moment. Barney takes one each for him and Leif since Leif's busy hugging him from behind and doesn't look like he's in a hurry to stop. Once Payne has their daughter planted firmly between them, he and Beau take their glasses too. Heath takes his and Griff's from where he's perched on Griff's lap. Orson and Ford are next. Keller and Will. Me and Mack. The final two are taken by Art and Joey.

"Thanks for taking this moment," Art says, none of his usual fuckery detected in his voice. "I don't know what it is about this year, but I've been more sentimental than usual lately." He shrugs, and Joey rubs his back softly. "I'm sitting here, looking around at your ugly faces, and realizing, somehow, I love you guys more than just about anyone in the world."

"Me, more than the rest of you," Joey points out.

"Thank fuck for that," Payne mutters.

"So thank you for being here," Art continues like there was no interruption. "Truly. Barney and I had a mad little idea, and it warms my heart to see how far it's come. How many of you have found your person. Knowing I've been able to be there for every one of you … it really is …" He blinks quickly. "Thank you for giving me that."

There's a stunned silence, and then Art cracks a smile.

"Now that I've officially freaked you all out …" He lifts his shot glass. "To us. Cheers."

"Cheers." We all throw back our drinks, and when I'm putting mine down, my gaze catches on where Mack is watching me.

"You okay?" I ask him.

"I think there's something in my eye."

Art roars with laughter. "I made Mack cry. Yes. I knew I'd get one of you."

Keller flicks a coaster at his head.

"Baby." I wrap my arm around him and squish him to my side. "I know … Art makes me cry as well."

Orson is still gaping at Art. "If this wasn't already a national holiday, I'd suggest it be made one. That was the most emotive he's been … ever. I think."

"There was also that time two years ago when he thought Joey was dying," Keller says.

Joey lights up. "Turns out he just forgot how many moles I have."

But no matter how much we tease him, Art holds this group together. He looked out for Mack when I couldn't, and he supported us both, separately through our divorce and now through our marriage. Art's emotional side might be rarely vocalized, but we all witness it. Every day.

I'll forever be grateful for his friendship. For all of theirs.

Over the last five years, our friends have gotten married, had kids, opened businesses, traveled, started whole new lives together. There's something about being in my forties that gives me a freedom in life that I've never had before. We all do.

The Divorced Men's Club might have been a way to stop us from feeling alone in the world, but I really have found a family with these guys, and I know if any of them needed me for anything, I'd be there.

Mack's lips press to the spot behind my ear. "I love you," he whispers, and it unleashes the kind of pure smile that our divorce took from me.

Life still isn't easy. It's a juggle with him managing the library full-time, with Van wanting to play every after-school sport under the sun and Kiera making a first-division basketball team, and me still having to travel for work.

But we're happy.

Genuinely happy.

Even five years later, that hasn't changed.

"The fireworks are about to start," Ford points out, and we all head downstairs into the parking lot of Killer Brew. We find Kiera and Van, hugging them between us while they still let us, and wait for the show to start.

From the first one that whistles out of Kil Pen and explodes with a crackle of color, contentment wraps around me.

No matter where in the world I've been, no matter the places I've seen and the people I've met, nothing beats this.

Family, friends, this tiny little town.

It's home.

And I wouldn't give it up for the world.

THANK YOU SO MUCH FOR READING THIS SERIES!

Want to know what I have in store next? I have early chapters, character art, and bonus content here:

https://geni.us/saxonpatreon

If you're looking for the next series of mine to jump into, the Accidental Love series features Keller's son Molly and his disastrous roommates.
Grab The Husband Hoax here.

AUTHOR'S NOTE

Thanks so much for reading these gorgeous guys!

The fact you keep showing up for me, release after release, means the absolute world! My dream has always been to have a career as an author and it's mind-blowing to me that I get to live it.

If you're a lover of signed paperbacks, special editions, audiobooks or merch, don't forget to check out my store.

You can find it through the link or QR code: www.saxon-jamesauthor.com

MY FREEBIES

Do you love friends to lovers?
Second chances or fake relationships?
I have two bonus freebies available!

Friends with Benefits
Total Fabrication
Making Him Mine

This short story is only available to my reader list so follow the
below and join the gang!

https://www.subscribepage.com/saxonjames

OTHER BOOKS BY SAXON JAMES

ACCIDENTAL LOVE SERIES:

Christian and Émile:

The Husband Hoax

Seven and Molly:

Not Dating Material

Rush and Hunter:

The Revenge Agenda

Madden and Penn:

Just Bromantically Invested

FRAT WARS SERIES:

Chad and Bailey:

Frat Wars: King of Thieves

Robbie and Brandon:

Frat Wars: Master of Mayhem

Zeke and Charles:

Frat Wars: Presidential Chaos

DIVORCED MEN'S CLUB SERIES:

Beau and Payne:

Roommate Arrangement

Griff and Heath:

Platonic Rulebook

Ford and Orson:

Budding Attraction

Art and Joey:

Employing Patience

Will and Keller:

System Overload

Mack and Davey:

Forgotten Romance

NEVER JUST FRIENDS SERIES:

Roo and Tanner:

Just Friends

Rowan and Circus:

Fake Friends

Auggie and Leon:

Getting Friendly

Cam and Rafe:

Friendly Fire

Reynolds and Arlo:

Bonus Short: Friends with Benefits

RECKLESS LOVE SERIES:

Denial

Risky

Tempting

CU HOCKEY SERIES WITH EDEN FINLEY:

Zach and Foster:

Power Plays & Straight A's

Beck and Jacobs:

Face Offs & Cheap Shots

Seth and Cohen:

Goal Lines & First Times

Asher and Kole:

Line Mates & Study Dates

West and Jasper:

Puck Drills & Quick Thrills

PUCKBOYS SERIES WITH EDEN FINLEY:

Ezra and Anton:

Egotistical Puckboy

Dex and Tripp:

Irresponsible Puckboy

Oskar and Lane:

Shameless Puckboy

Aleks and Gabe:

Foolish Puckboy

Vance and Quinn:

Clueless Puckboy

Miles and Bilson:

Bromantic Puckboy

Easton and Knox:

Forbidden Puckboy

STAND ALONES WITH EDEN FINLEY:

Remi and Sanden:

Up in Flames

Wren and Darcy:

The Bastard and The Heir

FRANKLIN U SERIES (VARIOUS AUTHORS):

Felix and Marshall:

The Dating Disaster

Benny and Harrison:

A Stealthy Situation

And if you're after something a little sweeter, don't forget my YA pen name

S. M. James.

These books are chock full of adorable, flawed characters with big hearts.

https://geni.us/smjames

WANT MORE FROM ME?

Follow Saxon James on any of the platforms below.
www.saxonjamesauthor.com
www.facebook.com/thesaxonjames/
www.amazon.com/Saxon-James/e/B082TP7BR7
www.bookbub.com/profile/saxon-james
www.instagram.com/saxonjameswrites/

ACKNOWLEDGMENTS

As with any book, this one took a hell of a lot of people to make happen.

The cover was created by the talented Rebecca at Story Styling Cover Designs with a gorgeous image by Wander Aguiar, and edits were done by Sandra Dee at One Love Editing, with Lori Parks proofreading the bejeebus out of it.

Thanks to Tal Lewin, @caravaggia13 on IG for creating amazing artworks for my website editions.

Charity VanHuss you're the most amazing PA I could have ever dreamed up. Without you I'd be even more of a chaotic disaster and there isn't enough space to list the many hats you wear for me. Paige and Lara Janz, you round out my team in the most incredible way and I'm always excited to see what fun ideas you both have next.

Eden Finley, thank you for being there for all the doubt spirals and hand-holding. Whether you wanted to be or not.
AM Johnson and Riley Hart thank you so much for taking the time to read. Your support is incredible and I really appreciate it!

And of course, thanks to my fam bam. To my husband who constantly frees up time for me to write, and to my kids whose neediness reminds me the real word exists.